ONE WEEK in PARADISE

Anise Starre is a born and bred Londoner who now travels the world with her husband. She loves writing sweet, fluffy romances featuring Black women being loved on and adored, with a hint of steam and spice to get the heart going. *One Week in Paradise* is her debut novel and the first book in the Flights and Feelings series. The second book is *One Last Job* and *One More Shot* is the third and final novel in the series.

You can follow Anise on Instagram @authoranisestarre and TikTok @anisestarre. Her website is anisestarre.com.

Also by Anise Starre

One Last Job
One More Shot

ONE WEEK in PARADISE

Anise Starre

SIMON & SCHUSTER

London · New York · Amsterdam/Antwerp · Sydney/Melbourne · Toronto · New Delhi

First published in Great Britain by Anise Starre, 2023
This edition published in Great Britain by Simon & Schuster UK Ltd, 2025

Copyright © Anise Starre, 2023

The right of Anise Starre to be identified as author
of this work has been asserted in accordance with the
Copyright, Designs and Patents Act, 1988.

1 3 5 7 9 10 8 6 4 2

Simon & Schuster UK Ltd
1st Floor
222 Gray's Inn Road
London WC1X 8HB

For more than 100 years, Simon & Schuster has championed authors and the stories they create. By respecting the copyright of an author's intellectual property, you enable Simon & Schuster and the author to continue publishing exceptional books for years to come. We thank you for supporting the author's copyright by purchasing an authorised edition of this book.

No amount of this book may be reproduced or stored in any format, nor may it be uploaded to any website, database, language-learning model, or other repository, retrieval, or artificial intelligence system without express permission. All rights reserved. Enquiries may be directed to Simon & Schuster, 222 Gray's Inn Road, London WC1X 8HB or RightsMailbox@simonandschuster.co.uk

Simon & Schuster Australia, Sydney
Simon & Schuster India, New Delhi

www.simonandschuster.co.uk
www.simonandschuster.com.au
www.simonandschuster.co.in

The authorised representative in the EEA is Simon & Schuster Netherlands BV,
Herculesplein 96, 3584 AA Utrecht, Netherlands. info@simonandschuster.nl

Simon & Schuster strongly believes in freedom of expression and stands against censorship in all its forms. For more information, visit BooksBelong.com

A CIP catalogue record for this book
is available from the British Library

Paperback ISBN: 978-1-3985-4412-3
eBook ISBN: 978-1-3985-4413-0

This book is a work of fiction. Names, characters, places and incidents
are either a product of the author's imagination or are used fictitiously.
Any resemblance to actual people living or dead,
events or locales is entirely coincidental.

Typeset in Bembo by Palimpsest Book Production Limited, Falkirk, Stirlingshire
Printed and Bound in the UK using 100% Renewable Electricity
at CPI Group (UK) Ltd

This is for those who don't believe love is something they deserve; that finding love is out of their reach.

But I'm here to tell you that you do deserve it; we all need more love in this world — it's just a matter of timing.

xo

Chapter One

My best friend has just bought a house.

My phone doesn't stop buzzing as she bombards our chat with photos and videos. I groan and shove my phone under my pillow. Sorry, Amber, but there are only so many heart-eye emojis I can send in a row. Does that make me a bad friend? Probably. Just another thing to add to the ever-growing list of things I'm bad at. Just like dancing, swimming, relationships, and unfortunately, *my job*.

Do I even have a job anymore? Hm. Debatable. Dad says I've never had a job, but he's always been like that. Mum used to be supportive, but I think that well has officially run dry.

Can you blame her? I'm twenty-seven years old and back in my childhood bedroom. Though I suppose I can't even call it that anymore. Mum and Dad have been using it as an office slash gym slash storage room for the last five years.

Cardboard boxes take up most of the floor space, and there's a treadmill in the corner with a thin layer of dust over it. The only things that remain from my tenure in here are my bed (now far too small – my feet are hanging off the end) and a Harry Styles poster I superglued to the wall when I was sixteen.

My phone buzzes again, and I resist the urge to fling it out the window.

God. How is this my life? Three months ago, I was living my very best life in London. I had my own riverside apartment, I was constantly on the go, my wardrobe was brimming with designer clothes, and I had a boyfriend who adored me.

Now I'm back living at my parents' house. I haven't stepped foot outside in a week, I'm living out of a pile of suitcases, and don't even get me started on the whole boyfriend thing. Life comes at you fast.

The buzzing finally starts to get to me. I grab my phone.

AMBER
37 new messages

I hover over our chat but then decide against opening it. Instead, I reflexively launch Instagram and immediately regret it – 230,000 followers. Last week it was 235,000. I'm losing followers at breakneck speed, and I don't know how to fix it.

In case you haven't guessed yet, I'm an influencer. Or should that be, 'I *used* to be an influencer'?

I was pretty good at it too. Don't get me wrong, I wasn't on Kim K or Molly Mae's level or anything like that, but I was doing pretty well for myself. I had a pretty decent and engaged following, and I had a long list of brands who were fighting to work with me. And they paid really well too. Enough for my expensive apartment in the city, multiple international trips a year, and pretty much anything else I wanted.

But that's all gone now. And all it took was one 45-second video. My stomach churns as I remember The Video. It's been three months, but I can't get it out of my head. I've committed every last painful second to memory, and it plays on a loop in my mind whenever I have a quiet moment.

'*Bailey?*'

For once, the sound of Mum's shrill voice yelling my name doesn't annoy me. It's a welcome distraction from The Video.

'Bailey, come down and eat something! I've made some sandwiches for lunch.' A pause, and then, 'You can't stay in there all day, you know?'

Part of me – a very big part of me – wants to prove her wrong. I *can* stay in here all day. I'm safe in my room, far away from Mum's worried stare and Dad's judgemental gaze. But then my stomach grumbles, and I know I'm fighting a losing battle.

'Coming!' I yell back. 'Give me five minutes.' I roll out of bed and rush into the bathroom opposite my room. It's a mess in here. Must remember to give it a clean before I give Mum something else to complain about. *God*. It's like I'm sixteen all over again.

I splash some water on my face and recoil as I catch a glimpse of my reflection in the mirror. I look awful. My long dark-brown curls are tangled and matted like a bird's nest, my eyes are bloodshot, and my cheeks look swollen from all the crying. It's no wonder Ethan hasn't tried to contact me.

That horrible feeling in the pit of my stomach is back as my thoughts drift to Ethan. My boyfriend. My *ex*-boyfriend.

Nope! I will not let my mind dwell on Ethan or The Video. Not if I can help it. I splash some more water on my face and quickly brush my teeth. I do what I can with my hair (hint: not much) and settle for pulling it into a messy bun before I slope downstairs.

'Ah, she has arisen!' Dad says as we pass in the hallway. He pretends to look shocked. 'I was about five minutes away from coming up there to check your pulse.'

'Ha ha,' I deadpan. 'Good morning to you too.'

'It's gone midday,' he says, following me into the kitchen. 'You can't spend all day in bed, Bailey. You need to get out there and find a job.'

'I have a job,' I say through gritted teeth. And it's true. I am technically still an influencer. It's just that, for reasons outside my control, I don't currently have the ability to influence anyone.

'You need a job that pays,' Dad says curtly. 'If you're going to stay here, I need to see you trying.'

I blink back tears and avoid his gaze by rifling through the cupboards to find my favourite tea blend – wild berry. How can he not see I'm trying? That I've *been* trying?

Even before this whole mess happened, Dad was never supportive of my influencer career. He wanted me to go to university and study medicine, just like he did. I had the grades for it, but I was never passionate about it.

'What's passion got to do with it?' Dad yelled at me when I told him I didn't want to go to university.

But what's life without passion? That's how I fell into influencing. I started off simply by sharing my natural hair journey on YouTube and Instagram. Growing up, it had always been difficult to find inspirational women on the internet who looked like me and understood my hair type. And don't even get me started on the struggle to find products that worked with my hair.

So I started my channel, *The Curly Bailey*, and it turned out that a lot of other young women resonated with me. I'd created a small but thriving community – a safe space for girls and women who look like me. And I was proud of it. I felt proud when young girls slid into my DMs telling me they'd never considered their hair or skin beautiful before, but my videos and posts had started them on a journey of self-love. Although my parents didn't understand it, I knew that what I was doing was important and necessary, and it gave me a sense of purpose.

My small community continued to grow and, before I knew it, hair brands were in my DMs, desperate to send me their products to review or book me for social media campaigns. I started branching out into make-up and fashion, and soon enough, *@TheCurlyBailey* was a hot commodity on the influencer scene.

Not anymore, though.

'Thanks for the pep talk, Dad,' I mumble as I make myself a cup of tea, then flee into the living room before he can say anything else.

Mum is sitting on the couch with a spread of tiny sandwiches on the coffee table in front of her.

'Hello, darling,' she says distractedly as I plop down next to her. She's absentmindedly watching the television, where a blonde woman is gingerly poking at a definitely undercooked chicken.

'*Come Dine with Me*?' I ask.

Mum hums in acknowledgement. 'She's making chicken *francese*. Or she's trying to, at least.'

We watch in silence and eat our sandwiches for a few minutes as the blonde woman (Julie, according to the presenter) burns the chicken. Then Mum turns to me and smiles, but it's not a good smile.

'So,' she says, delicately folding her hands in her lap.

'Mum,' I groan. 'Please don't start. I just got it from Dad.'

'I'm not going to start,' sniffs Mum. 'I'm just— *We're* just worried about you, darling. You turn up at our door crying, telling us you've lost your apartment and that you've broken up with sweet Ethan.'

Sweet Ethan. I snort. She doesn't know how wrong she is.

'And then you tell us we're not allowed to ask any questions,' Mum continues. 'You can't expect us not to worry.'

She's right – I know she is. But I can't bring myself to tell them what happened. I wouldn't be able to bear the shame. Thankfully, I'm spared from having to answer by the sound of the front door being flung open.

'Anyone home?' yells my big brother, Dane.

I say 'big brother' but Dane is only two years older than me, and our age gap has begun to feel smaller the older we get. To me, anyway. Ask him, and I'll always be his baby sister.

Mum leaps up from the couch as soon as she hears his voice. I roll my eyes. Dane has always been her favourite. I used to be Dad's favourite, but I've not held that title in a very long time.

'Darling,' Mum coos as Dane pops his head around the living-room door.

Growing up, people used to think we were twins, and I can see why. We're both brown-skinned, with thick, curly dark brown hair, though Dane's hair is now in long locs that fall to the middle of his back. I once posted a photo of us together on Instagram, and it got more likes and heart-eye emojis than anything I'd ever posted before. Girls love Dane, and he knows it.

He embraces Mum in a tight hug and shoots me an inquisitive look. I bite my lip.

Dane isn't on social media. He has a Facebook account he made back when it first came out, and then he never touched it again, but that's about it. The chances of him having seen The Video are low, but not zero. I'll have to approach this with caution.

'Hey,' I say coolly as he pulls me into a one-armed hug. 'What're you doing here?'

'Checking out the space for the conservatory,' he explains.

'The conservatory?' I ask.

'Didn't I tell you?' Mum jumps in. Her eyes are dancing with excitement. 'Dane's offered to do our conservatory for us. An early anniversary present.'

Ah. That makes sense. I feel a twinge of jealousy but quickly brush it away. Dane didn't go to university either, but Dad didn't mind. Instead, he did an apprenticeship at a construction company and eventually started his own. Great Dane Construction Services. The logo even has a little cartoon dog on it, with its tongue poking out. I thought it was kind of cringey when he first showed me the logo, but he's done incredibly well for himself. Much better than I have. I'm proud of him, no matter how much it stings right now.

'Yeah,' says Dane. 'Cash is just parking the van round the corner.'

'Cash?' I squeak. 'Cash is here? Why?'

Cash – short for Caspian – is my brother's best friend turned business partner and has been nothing but a thorn in my side since we were all teenagers. I don't know why, but he's never liked me. I guess he's always just seen me as Dane's annoying little sister, who used to follow them around and snitch on them whenever they did anything vaguely dangerous or refused to let me hang out with them. He's not outwardly rude or anything, but he avoids me like the plague. Which suits me just fine. He's an ass who, for some reason, thinks he's better than everyone else. Especially me.

But I suppose that's what happens when you're unnecessarily and ridiculously good-looking – you don't have to develop a personality.

I told you that girls love Dane, but it's nothing compared to the attention Cash gets from them. Growing up, all my friends – hell, all the girls at my school – were obsessed with him. I can't tell you how many times a girl would approach me and beg me to give Cash their number. I never did.

'He's helping with the conservatory,' Dane says with a shrug, like it's the most obvious thing in the world. Which, to be fair, it is. Cash joined Great Dane Construction Services in the early days, and the two regularly team up for projects.

'Such a sweet boy,' says Mum with a fond smile. 'How are things going with—'

'Hi, Mrs Clarke.'

We all jump. I hadn't even heard the front door open again, but Cash is suddenly in front of us, standing in the doorway to the living room.

All six foot four of him towers over Mum as he pulls her into an easy hug. He's wearing an old Great Dane Construction Services T-shirt that clings to his torso and shows off his lean yet muscular arms and a pair of grey sweatpants that hang low on his hips. The waistband of his boxer shorts peeks out, showing off a cheeky splash of bright blue. I look up and, to my alarm, discover that Cash is staring directly at me.

His eyes – an unusual blend of grey and green – narrow as he runs a hand through his chin-length black, wavy locks.

'Bailey,' he says curtly. His brows furrow in what I can only assume is annoyance at the sight of me.

'Hi, Cash,' I say as brightly as I can, shooting him my sweetest smile. Just because he's an ass doesn't mean that I have to be, does it? And besides, I'm all for taking the high road, especially when it results in Cash looking visibly taken aback by my cheery tone. *Ha.* Take that, asshole.

His gaze roves over me, and for some reason, I'm suddenly acutely aware of just how awful I look right now. I'm still in my pyjamas, wearing an oversized Care Bears T-shirt that has *Hug Life* printed across the front and a pair of Ethan's old boxer shorts.

'I'm gonna go and get dressed,' I say as I shuffle past him. Nobody hears me, though. Mum is busy pulling Dane and Cash towards the sliding doors at the back of the living room to show them where she wants the conservatory to go.

I glance back at Cash before I disappear upstairs. He's laughing politely at something Mum's said, and I can't help but notice he's got a fantastic smile.

Cash is the kind of guy who's just effortlessly good-looking. It doesn't surprise me at all that he's constantly got girls drooling over him. Hell, if his personality wasn't so *bleugh*, I'd probably be into him too.

Chapter Two

'And this is the en suite.' Amber's grinning face disappears as she flips her phone's camera around to show me the large en suite bathroom that connects to her bedroom.

After I showered and put on some real clothes, I finally plucked up the courage to call Amber back. If she's annoyed by my slow responses, she doesn't let it show. As soon as she picks up the call, she launches into a whirlwind tour of her new home.

'I have a garden!' she squeals, pressing her phone up against the window so I can see the patch of green behind her new home. 'It's tiny, but I have a *garden*! I can't wait for BBQ season.'

'Amber, you can't cook,' I remind her. The girl is a mess in the kitchen.

'Maybe I'll have a hot, strapping man by then to cook for me,' Amber says with a dreamy sigh.

I snort. 'How very feminist of you.'

'Hey!' Amber laughs. 'Give me a break. I just bought a house by myself. If that's not the most badass feminist thing, then I don't know what is.'

She's right. Amber is twenty-eight years old and, as of today, has climbed aboard the property ladder without any help. I'm so incredibly proud of her.

Amber is the kind of person who, when she sets a goal, you can be damn sure that she's going to hit it. When she announced, three years ago over happy hour cocktails in some dingy South London bar, that she was going to buy herself her dream home in the suburbs of London in four years or less, everyone at the table laughed at her. But not me. I knew that she was going to do it. She's the very definition of kick-ass.

She's an interior designer with a long list of rich and famous clients who keep her booked and busy. She's my best friend, but we haven't seen each other face to face since before The Video because her schedule is so hectic.

'Anyway,' she says, flipping the camera back to her face as she flops down onto a beanbag – the sole piece of furniture she currently has in her new living room. 'How're you? Good to see you're wearing proper clothes today.'

The *Hug Life* T-shirt has been replaced by a simple white tank top. Nothing special, but I do look less haggard.

'About the same as yesterday,' I say with what I hope is a casual shrug. 'It's . . . it's hard.'

'I know, babe,' says Amber softly. 'I just want to give you

a big hug. Once I've got some actual furniture, you need to come over for a week-long sleepover. Or you could come now if you want, but we'll be sleeping on the floor.'

I'm grateful for the offer, but truth be told, I've been avoiding Amber ever since The Video. I know she'd never judge me, but I can't help but feel like such a failure.

'I'll wait for the furniture to come,' I say.

There's a brief pause, and I can see Amber is gearing up to say something. She has a tell. When she's anxious about something, she always starts playing with her hair. I watch as she twists one of her wavy locks around her finger and wait patiently for her to get the words out.

'You still haven't posted,' she says quickly. 'Not since . . . well. You know.'

I grimace. To her credit, Amber has deftly avoided the topic almost entirely for the last three months, so I can't be mad that she's finally brought it up.

'Don't be mad,' she says quickly. 'I just don't want you to lose everything you've worked so hard for.'

'I've already lost it,' I mumble.

Amber scoffs. 'Bailey. Stop being ridiculous. You still have over *two hundred thousand followers.*'

Actually it's 229,823 now. I checked in a moment of weakness after hopping out of the shower.

'You need to post something again,' she continues. 'Get back out there. Show everyone that you're still a boss bitch.'

She gets another snort out of me for that.

'I promise, as soon as you start posting again, the brands will be sliding into your DMs like none of this ever happened.'

'It's not the brands I'm worried about,' I say. 'It's the comments.'

After The Video went viral, the comments under all my posts were a toxic mess. I tried my best to ignore them for as long as I could, but after a week or so of casually being told to kill myself every few minutes, I had to turn the comments off. That was hard. It felt like I was letting the trolls win.

'But, babe,' she says, fiddling with her hair again, 'don't you think this radio silence makes you look kind of guilty? I know you're not,' she adds quickly, accurately deciphering the look of annoyance that must flit across my face. 'But *they* don't. They saw The Video, and then you didn't say anything. You didn't even try and defend yourself.'

'You told me not to!' I say defensively.

'I told you not to say anything in the heat of the moment,' Amber clarifies. 'You were supposed to sit and think about your response so you didn't say anything you might regret. I didn't think you'd go completely silent.'

She continues talking, but my attention is elsewhere. An email notification has popped up at the top of my phone. The preview reads:

YOU AND I COUPLES RESORT – PRESS INVITE

My stomach does a funny little flip. *That's an invitation from a brand.* It's been months since I last got one of these. I quickly tap on the email, ignoring Amber's irritated 'Did you just put me on pause?'

From: Penelope Smith <penelope@youandiresort.com>
To: Bailey Clarke <bailey@thecurlybailey.com>
Subject: YOU AND I COUPLES RESORT – PRESS INVITE

Dear Bailey,

I hope this email finds you well. I'm writing as we'd love to extend an all-inclusive invite to the brand new You and I resort in Jamaica to you and your partner. We're huge fans of your content and would love to host you at the resort later this month for a week. We have an exciting schedule of activities planned for the week and will, of course, give yourself and your partner plenty of time to explore the resort as you desire. We do hope you'll be able to join us. Please let me know by Friday if this will be possible, as we need to move quickly with flights.

Best wishes,
Penelope

'Oh. My. God.'

'What? What? What?' Amber shouts.

'I just got an invite email from a brand,' I tell her. My heart is racing. 'They want to fly me out to Jamaica to their resort.'

Amber's screech is deafening. 'Bailey! What did I tell you? Jamaica? This is amazing.'

'Don't get too excited,' I interrupt her imminent rant about what I'll need to pack. 'I'm not going.'

Amber's smile drops from her face. 'What the fuck? Why not?'

'Well, it's more like I can't go,' I say. 'It's a *couples resort*.' I read her the email and shrug. 'See? They mustn't have got the memo about me and Ethan.'

They must not have seen The Video.

I feel a sting in my chest as I think about Ethan. I've done such a good job of pushing him out of my mind up until now. I let out a dry laugh. It figures that the first opportunity I get post-break-up would rely completely on us being a couple.

'Oh, babe,' Amber says softly. 'I'm sorry. But look at it like this. If this brand wants you, so many more will. This is why you need to start posting again.'

She's right. I know she is, but I can't bring myself to post just yet. My stomach turns in knots as I imagine the flood of hateful comments that will likely come in the second I post anything.

'You need to move forward,' Amber says firmly. 'Show them that you've got nothing to hide.'

I swallow. Amber knows almost everything there is to know about me. But she doesn't know this.

I do have something to hide.

Chapter Three

Dinner is an incredibly awkward affair because, on Mum's insistence, Cash is still here. He's seated directly opposite me, and aside from a small grimace when I first entered the room, he's paid me no attention whatsoever.

To be honest, that suits me just fine. I can't stop thinking about the email and just how unfair life is. All I want to do is run back up to my room, crawl into a ball, and cry. But Dad insisted I come down and join them for dinner, so here I am.

I stab at my spaghetti, scratching the plate slightly with my fork. I drown out the sound of conversation around the table, my mind swirling with thoughts of Ethan and what he's doing right now. Does he miss me? Probably not.

The thoughts unsettle me slightly. I don't *want* to think about him, but they keep pushing to the forefront of my mind without permission. After everything Ethan's put me through, why do I even miss him?

'. . . sure you could find something for her. What do you think, Bailey?'

I snap back to reality and realise that everyone is staring at me. Even Cash. I catch his gaze for half a second before he glances away, his lips dipping slightly into a frown.

'Did you hear me, Bailey?' Dad asks.

'No, sorry,' I say. 'I must've zoned out. What're we talking about?'

'You,' says Dad sharply. 'And Dane. He may be able to get you a job.'

I grip my fork tightly. 'Dad, I already told you. I have a job.'

Out of the corner of my eye, I can see Mum pretending to be interested in a random spot on the ceiling to avoid getting involved. *Thanks for the support, Mum.*

'And I've already told you, you need to get a job that actually pays you,' he says. 'When was the last time you earned any money from this Instagram nonsense?'

Nonsense? I squeeze my fork even tighter. The metal is going to leave a groove in the palm of my hand if I don't stop soon.

'Dad,' Dane says softly. 'We don't need to do this now. Me and Bailey can talk about work later.'

'No, we can't,' I say through gritted teeth. 'Because I don't need *you* to give me a job.'

I know my anger is misplaced. That Dane has probably been blindsided by Dad just as much as I have. But I don't care.

'Things have been difficult recently,' I say slowly. 'Yes, that's true. But I'm fine. I don't need anyone's pity.'

Cash shifts awkwardly in front of me. He's desperately trying to avoid catching my gaze again. Why is this happening in front of *him*?

'We don't pity you, darling,' Mum says, finally deciding to throw me a bone. 'We're just worried about you. You're not yourself lately. And you still haven't told us about what happened between you and sweet Ethan.'

Sweet Ethan *again*.

'Have you thought about the fact that Ethan maybe wasn't so sweet?' I snap.

Mum recoils slightly at the venom in my tone, and guilt washes over me.

'Sorry,' I mumble. 'I just need some time.'

'How much time do you need?' Dad says sharply. 'You've been here for two weeks, and you've barely left the house. We've tried to be compassionate, but you need to come back to the real world.'

If this is what compassion is, I don't want to see Dad's idea of tough love.

'What's happened with the influencer thing?' Dane asks, looking genuinely confused. I allow a wave of relief to wash over me. He definitely hasn't seen The Video. 'I thought you were smashing it?'

'I was. I mean, I am,' I say defensively. 'It's going great.

In fact, just today, a brand reached out and offered to fly me to Jamaica for a week.'

The words fall from my lips before I can even register what I'm saying. I can't help but feel a little smug when I notice the way Dad's thick eyebrows shoot up into his hairline.

'Jamaica?' Dane whistles. He shoots me an impressed nod. 'When are you flying out?'

The smugness disappears almost instantly. I clear my throat and say, as casually as I can, 'I'm not going to go, actually.'

'Why?' Dad asks. 'You've got something else to be doing?'

I scowl at him. Why is he being so mean?

'No, it's just . . . well, the trip is only for couples,' I admit reluctantly. 'And since Ethan and I have broken up, I can't really go, can I?'

A very painful silence blankets the table. Aside from The Video going viral, I don't think I've ever been more embarrassed. I move to push myself away from the dining table, but before I can flee upstairs, Dane clears his throat.

'You could still go,' he says with a nonchalant shrug.

'I'm pretty sure they don't want my single ass there depressing all the happy couples,' I mutter.

'So take someone,' he says, like it's the most obvious thing in the world. 'Does it say in the email that you have to bring Ethan specifically?'

'No,' I say slowly. 'But I don't have anyone to bring. I'm not exactly on the market right now.'

For a brief moment I consider trawling through Tinder or Hinge to find someone to take with me, but I quickly dismiss the idea. I can't think of anything worse.

'Bring a friend,' he says. His lips curl into a sly grin. 'Hell, bring Cash.'

I can't think of anything worse – except maybe *that*.

Cash's head whips around so fast I'm surprised his neck doesn't snap.

'Dane, I don't—' Cash begins, but Dane is on a roll.

'Yeah, you and Cash should go!' Dane says excitedly. 'Listen, you both need a break.'

I glance at Cash. There's a light pink dusting slowly blooming on his cheeks. He's still not caught my gaze.

'And what better place to rest and relax than Jamaica?' Dane asks. He shoots Cash a devilish smirk.

Dad rolls his eyes. 'This is ridiculous. She doesn't need a holiday – she needs a job!'

'I think it sounds like a lovely idea,' Mum says loudly, cutting across Dad. She offers me a warm smile, and a wave of gratitude washes over me. 'Dane's right, sweetheart. I don't know what's happened, and I'll be here when you're ready to talk about it, but you clearly need a break. Go to Jamaica, get your head straight, and then come back ready to get going again.'

That does sound very enticing, but . . .

'I'm sure Cash doesn't want to spend a week with me,'

I say. And *I* definitely don't want to spend a week with him. No doubt he'd cast a gloomy and grumpy shadow over my tropical paradise.

'Nah, he'd love to,' Dane says, still wearing that smirk. 'Like I said, you both need a break. Cash has been working like mad recently, and with everything that's happening with—'

'The conservatory,' Cash cuts in suddenly. He shoots Dane a look I can't quite decipher, but it looks relatively similar to the one Amber and I share if we want the other to stop talking for some reason when we're with other people. 'With everything that's happening with the conservatory, I'll have some free time.'

What?

Is Cash actually considering this? The man who, for all the time I've known him, has made it his personal mission to ignore me is *actually* considering this?

It's not that I don't want to go to Jamaica. This is the biggest opportunity to slide into my inbox since way before The Video, and I don't want to turn it down. But it's *Cash*. Has he ever even thrown a friendly glance my way? I genuinely don't think he has.

It won't be all bad, though, I think to myself. Surely we won't have to spend *all* our time together? I think back to what Amber said earlier. I know she's right. I do need to start posting again, and this trip could be the perfect way to start rebuilding my brand.

And, as terrible as this sounds, I'm not entirely opposed to the idea of showing up with someone who looks like Cash on my arm.

Hold on.

Am *I* considering this now?

Dane nods eagerly. 'Exactly. We've got to order some equipment in for the job, and it won't be here for a while.'

I bite my lip and glance over at Cash. For the first time, he actually meets my gaze. His grey-green eyes lock in on me, and I feel something stir in the pit of my stomach.

'I, uh . . . I wouldn't mind going,' he says quickly, like he needs to get the words out fast before he regrets them. He scratches at the perpetual five o'clock stubble on his chin. 'If you don't mind, that is.'

A week of pretending to be dating Caspian Reid.

I weigh up my options. Option one: stay at home, basking in my misery and hiding from the world in the hopes that they'll forget about The Video.

Option two: Go to Jamaica, face my fears head on and spend the week pretending that Cash is my adoring boyfriend.

I take a deep breath and offer Cash a weak smile. 'Let's do it.'

* * *

'What the hell is wrong with you?' I whack Dane with one of Mum's fancy sofa cushions.

Dane cackles and expertly dives out of the way before I can continue my onslaught. 'I'm sure I have no idea what you're talking about.'

We're alone in the living room. Mum and Dad have gone up to bed, and Cash has taken an Uber home. We've made tentative plans to meet up next week to discuss our upcoming trip, and the thought of it fills me with anxiety.

'You know what you did!' I glower at my brother. 'Stop laughing. It's not funny.'

'It's actually very hilarious,' Dane snickers. 'I don't see what the big deal is. Do you not want to go to Jamaica?'

I roll my eyes. 'Of course I do.'

'Then what's the problem? You get a free holiday out of it. Cash gets a tan. It's a win-win situation in my book.'

'I don't know if you've noticed, but Cash isn't exactly my biggest fan.'

Dane pauses for a second before his eyes light up, and he throws his head back, roaring with laughter. '*What?*'

'What's so funny?' I scowl.

'Nothing, nothing. Don't worry about it.' His expression turns serious. 'So, are you gonna tell me what happened?'

'Nothing happened.'

'Bailey, come on,' he says. 'You broke up with Ethan. You're back home. Something happened.'

'You never liked Ethan anyway,' I say, hoping to steer the subject away from me. 'So you should be happy.'

'True. I hated the guy. He's such a snob. But, if he made you happy, then . . .' Dane shrugs. 'Tell me what happened, Bailey.'

There's something earnest in his expression that begins to chip at the carefully constructed walls I've put up.

'He was cheating on me,' I mumble. I avoid eye contact, blinking away tears. 'Was cheating the whole time.'

'Jesus, fuck.'

Dane scooches a little closer to me on the sofa and wraps an arm around my shoulders. I instinctively lean into him as the tears begin to fall.

'What a dickhead,' he mutters.

Despite everything, I can't help but laugh at that. 'Exactly.'

'But why're you back home?' he asks after letting me cry quietly for a minute or two.

I stiffen slightly and pull away. I'm not ready to talk about The Video and aftermath of it all just yet.

Dane seems to sense my hesitation, and he holds his hands up defensively in front of him. 'All right. I get it. Whenever you're ready to talk, I'm here.'

'You sound just like Mum.'

'Good.' Dane flashes me an easy smile. 'She's a wise woman.'

He dips into his pocket and pulls out his phone. On the lock screen, I can see notifications of unread messages from at least three different women. I roll my eyes.

'When are you going to stop being such a player?'

'Hm?' He looks genuinely confused. 'I don't know what you mean.'

Before I can probe any further, he opens up our chat history and fires off a quick message. My phone vibrates. He's sent me Cash's contact details.

'So you can message each other about the trip,' he says, and that sly smirk from the dinner table is back.

'I can't believe he agreed to it,' I say as I save Cash's number into my phone.

'Why wouldn't he?' Dane asks. 'Free trip to Jamaica. I wish I was going.'

'But he'll have to pretend to be my boyfriend,' I say, and I can feel my cheeks warming with each passing second. 'And even if you've never noticed it before, I *know* Cash doesn't like me.'

'You know nothing, Bailey Clarke,' Dane laughs. We recently went through a phase where we were both obsessed with *Game of Thrones*. 'Stop overthinking things. Go to Jamaica, get a tan, take some nice pictures, and bring me back a shell. And some rum.'

'I'll do my best,' I laugh.

Chapter Four

Dane and Cash have been best friends since they were eleven years old. That's about eighteen years now, and I think I could count the minutes I've spent alone with Cash on one hand.

We fly out on Saturday – Penelope wasn't lying when she said we need to move fast – and Cash and I have agreed to meet in a café today to discuss plans and ground rules. I'm already a nervous wreck, and it doesn't help that I'm running late. I got distracted by a call with Amber venting about a nightmare client she's currently dealing with.

I fire off a quick and apologetic message to Cash as I run up the high street. He responds in seconds with nothing but a thumbs-up emoji.

Oh God. He's pissed.

It takes me another seven minutes to find The Steam Room, the small and cosy café we've agreed to meet at.

Before I enter, I catch a glimpse of myself in the window. Not to toot my own horn, but I think I look pretty cute today.

It's the first time I've left the house in over a week and a half, and I've scrubbed up pretty well. I'm trialling a new shampoo and conditioner combo – gifted by a brand before The Video – and it's done wonders with my hair. My hair falls in ringlets around my face and has a picture-perfect shine to it. I don't think my hair has looked so healthy in months. A small part of me wants to take a picture right now and post it, but my anxiety outweighs my daring, and I resist the urge.

As I give my hair an extra bit of fluffing, I realise that someone is staring at me through the window.

Grey-green eyes meet mine, and I yelp. Cash is staring directly at me, his lips twisted into a smirk. He gestures to the empty seat in front of him and then glances at an imaginary watch on his wrist.

'Sorry,' I mouth before hurrying into The Steam Room. 'Sorry, sorry, sorry!' I say again as I plop down into the empty seat. 'I was helping a friend out, and I lost track of time.'

'It's no big deal,' Cash says. 'No need to apologise.'

He sounds sincere, but I know it's just a façade. I can tell by the way he's avoiding holding eye contact with me for more than a half second. He's definitely irritated with me.

'Well, let me get you something to drink,' I say. 'It's the least I can do.'

'Don't worry about it.' He gestures to the table between us. There's a big black teapot and two small cups beside it. 'I've already ordered for us. Wild berry, right?'

Surprise jolts through me as I watch him pour me a steaming cup of wild berry tea.

'Yeah,' I say. 'Thanks.'

He shrugs like it's the most normal thing in the world to know the tea preference of your best friend's younger sister.

We sit for a moment, quietly sipping our tea, and I take the opportunity to watch him. His wavy hair is pulled into a loose bun today, with a few wispy strands falling over his face. I'm suddenly overcome with the urge to run my fingers through his hair. I wonder if it's soft as it looks.

Cash clears his throat suddenly, and I realise I've been caught staring.

'So,' he says. 'Jamaica.'

'Jamaica,' I nod. 'Thanks again for agreeing to come with me.'

'Free trip to Jamaica. Who would say no?'

I wait for a moment, wondering if he'll fill in the pause with something like *'and the company's not too bad either'*, to assuage my fear that he doesn't actually like me. But no clarifier comes. He really is just in this for the free trip.

'Right,' I say, trying not to let the disappointment show

on my face. I clear my throat. 'Let's get down to business. Penelope's sent over an itinerary – I'll forward it to you later. They've got lots planned for us. For the most part, we can pick and choose which activities we'd like to do, but the resort is, um, focused on couples, so they'll be expecting us to do a few of the couples activities definitely.'

'Things like what?' Cash asks.

'Nothing big,' I say lightly, hoping my face isn't as red as it feels. 'Maybe a couples massage. Tandem jet-skiing. They've got dancing lessons at night as well, which I think Penelope is keen on us giving a go. Stuff like that.'

If the idea of us getting a couples massage or having my chest pressed up against his back while we zoom through the sea bothers him, Cash doesn't let it show. His face is a perfect mask of indifference.

'And you'll be taking photos and videos the whole time?' he asks. 'For your Instagram?'

I nod. 'Yes, exactly. I'm also going to make a vlog for my YouTube channel.'

'And I've got to be in all of them?'

There's something in his eyes when he says that. Is it panic? Regret? I can't tell.

'Not all of them,' I say. 'The resort will definitely want a few because we're going specifically to experience the *romantic* element, but we can get creative with the framing if you don't want your face to be in any of them.'

Secretly, I always think it's really cringe when people soft-launch their new partner by posting carefully taken photos and videos where the partner's face isn't showing. Up until all of three months ago, in between my hair, fashion and make-up posts, there were proud photos of Ethan and me littering my feed. I never tried to hide him. Maybe that's what made him so bold.

Cash shrugs. 'I don't mind being in a few. You'll let me see them before you post anything?'

'Of course. I won't post anything you're not happy with. And I won't tag you in anything.' A thought suddenly occurs to me. 'Are you even on Instagram?'

'Kind of,' he says. 'I have an account. A private account. I don't really post or use it very much.'

'Wow.' I don't know why this surprises me so much. 'You know, I assumed you'd be like Dane and have zero social media presence.'

'I might as well,' he says with a soft chuckle. 'Like I said, I don't really post much.'

'Can I see?' I ask. I'm intrigued.

He hesitates for a beat too long.

'Sorry,' I say. For a moment, I let myself forget what this was. We're not friends. Cash doesn't like me. 'You don't have to share it with me if you don't want to.'

'No, no. It's fine,' he says, pulling out his phone. He launches Instagram and shows me his screen.

The username @*CASHMONEY93* jumps out at me, and I can't turn my snort of laughter into a believable cough quickly enough.

'*Cash Money 93?*' I cackle. 'That is hilarious.'

Cash's cheeks are slightly redder than before. 'Yeah. Didn't think that one through.'

'You know you can change it, right?'

His eyes widen slightly. 'Seriously?'

My cackle turns into a full-blown laughing fit. 'You didn't know that your username isn't permanent?'

'No!' Cash groans, running a hand down his face. 'I assumed that it was a permanent kind of thing.'

'Pretend I never told you,' I say, still laughing. 'Never change it. It's maybe the funniest thing I've seen in weeks.'

Cash's face splits into quite possibly the widest smile I've ever seen on him. I don't know if it's the way the sun is hitting him or what, but he's mesmerising to look at in this moment.

'Then I'll keep it,' he says. He meets and holds my gaze. 'Just for you.'

My heart skips a beat, and I quickly look away. 'Thanks.'

We spend the next half an hour discussing our plans to meet on Saturday, and I give him a rundown of what to expect when we meet Penelope and the others.

'Others?' Cash asks, looking slightly alarmed.

'There will definitely be some other influencers and their partners coming on the trip,' I explain.

'I thought it would be just us,' he says. For some reason, he looks a little deflated.

'Very unlikely. There will probably be at least three other couples. The brand has to make sure they get the content they need on this trip. They can't rely entirely on just us.'

Cash nods. 'That makes sense.'

'Just to warn you, the other influencers might seem surprised to see you. My break-up with Ethan was pretty public.' And that's putting it nicely.

'That's fine. I can handle that.'

I wait to see if he's going to ask anything about Ethan, but nothing comes. His commitment to not caring about me at all is impressive in a weird, twisted way.

'I'll have to introduce you as my new boyfriend,' I say, tentatively. Cash drops his gaze once again. 'And they'll expect us to look the part.'

'What does that mean?'

I bite my lip. 'Nothing you wouldn't be comfortable with. Just play the part as best you can. I'm sure you've had plenty of practice.'

It suddenly occurs to me that I know nothing about Cash's dating history. Dane isn't the kind of brother to offer up that information unprompted, and I've never thought to ask. I wonder what kind of boyfriend he is.

'Is there anything *you* wouldn't be comfortable with?' he asks.

'We won't have to kiss or anything like that,' I say quickly. Maybe a bit too quickly because Cash quirks a brow. 'I just mean, you're my brother's best friend. I don't want to make anything weird.'

'Weirder than pretending to be your boyfriend to get a free trip to Jamaica?'

My lips twitch. At least he can see the humour in all of this. 'Exactly.'

'Got it,' he says. 'No kissing.'

'What about you?' I ask. 'Is there anything you wouldn't be comfortable with?'

Something stirs in the pit of my stomach as Cash looks me directly in the eye, licks his lips, and says, 'No.'

★ ★ ★

I'm lying in bed – feet hanging off the edge – when something suddenly hits me. I haven't followed Cash back on Instagram yet.

After we finished discussing our boundaries on the trip, we shared one more pot of tea before we parted ways. I'm pleasantly surprised by how easily the conversation flowed between us. I don't think we're on our way to becoming best friends or anything like that, but I think we've definitely taken a step in the right direction.

I fish out my phone, pull up Instagram and quickly type @CASHMONEY93 into the search bar. He comes up immediately, and, to my surprise, the little blue bar next to his profile picture says, '*FOLLOW BACK*'.

Cash is already following me.

I quickly flick through my notifications, but there's no sign of Cash there in the last few days. That means he's been following me for a while. I wonder why he didn't mention it.

I head back to his profile and press *FOLLOW BACK*. I only have to wait two minutes before I get another notification informing me that Cash has accepted my follow request.

Very speedy. I wasn't expecting a response so fast.

Cash wasn't lying when he said that he doesn't post much. There are only two posts on his feed. The oldest one, posted nearly ten years ago, is a photo of a sunset with a heavy Valencia filter over it.

The other one, posted last summer, is a photo of him and a group of friends standing beside a lake. They're all covered in mud from head to toe and have identical grins pasted across their faces. Dane is in the photo too.

I know where this photo is from. One of Dane and Cash's mutual friends got married last year, and they went on a muddy obstacle course for his stag do. Dane was complaining for weeks about all the mud in his hair.

My gaze drifts to Cash. He's wearing a criminally short pair of shorts, and his mud and water-drenched T-shirt clings to his torso, showing off his impressive form.

I'm not under any kind of delusion. Cash is hot. And we're about to spend the next week pretending to be a couple.

The thought makes my spine tingle.

I hover over the tagged pictures tab on his profile, suddenly desperate to see more of him, but a notification from Amber distracts me.

AMBER
> This client is driving me up the wall
>
> FaceTime?

I tap out of Instagram and quickly call Amber. She answers almost immediately with a long groan.

'If you suddenly stop hearing from me, I've probably been arrested for murder, and I'm in jail,' she says dramatically.

'What's going on?' I laugh.

'Remember Asshole Client?'

How could I forget? This man has been the bane of her life for the last six months. She doesn't wait for me to respond before she ploughs on.

'Well, he's reared his stupidly handsome head again. I don't think I've had a more indecisive client in my entire career. He hates everything I show him, even though it fits his brief to a *tee*. At this point, I'm starting to think he's being difficult on purpose.'

'At least you're getting paid,' I say.

'That's true,' she laughs. 'I've been charging him time and a half recently because what the fuck. Sometimes I think he's genuinely messing with me for fun.'

She rants for a little bit longer, alternating between calling him Asshole Client and Stupidly Handsome Dickhead. Interesting. *Very* interesting. I file this away to bring up later when she's less heated.

'Anyway,' she sighs after ten minutes. 'How're you doing? All ready for Jamaica?'

'Nearly. I've finished packing, and I met with Cash earlier today to talk about plans and boundaries.'

'Oooh,' Amber wiggles her brows. 'Boundaries, huh?'

'So things don't get weird. He's Dane's best friend. I'm not trying to ruin that.'

'That's fair,' says Amber. 'Have you thought about content? What's your first post gonna be?'

I have actually spent a lot of time thinking about that. 'I think I'll test it out with a few stories first. See what kind of response I get, and if it's not too bad, I'll maybe post something to the grid on day two or three.'

'You gonna post Cash?'

'Definitely not on the grid, but he'll make some kind of appearance in my stories for sure.' A tactical back-of-the-head shot or something similar.

'I hope Ethan sees it, and it sends him spiralling,' Amber

cackles. But I don't join her. Amber doesn't notice. 'Not to be a jerk, but Cash is a trillion times hotter than Ethan.'

'Mmm,' I hum noncommittally. I don't want to talk about Ethan. Besides, he's been blocked ever since The Video.

Amber spews some more Ethan hate – which usually I'd be all for – and then remembers she's got a pizza in the oven.

'Oh no. It's burnt.' She holds the pizza up in front of the camera, showing off a completely blackened circle.

'That's an understatement,' I laugh.

'I'm gonna go try and find something else to eat. Talk to you later, babe.' Amber blows me a kiss and then cuts the call.

I pull up Instagram again, this time to check my follower count (229,629 – ouch), but Cash's page is still up.

I'm not sure what comes over me, but I open up the stag do photo, and after a moment's hesitation, I double-tap it.

Chapter Five

My heart is in my throat as I wheel my suitcase through Gatwick Airport. I've barely slept, and I'm a bundle of nerves. Cash is supposed to be meeting me at the check-in counter, and I regret not deciding to meet him somewhere else.

Aside from double checking he knew where and when to meet, we haven't spoken since the café. The Cash I met in the café was nicer than the Cash I've known since we were children, and it lulled me into a false sense of security. Was there a chance that Cash was finally starting to get over his weird hang-up with me, and we could potentially be friends?

It's stupid, but I'd allowed myself to hope so.

After the café, I tried to keep up some friendly conversation, even going so far as to send him a cheesy photo of me sitting on top of my overflowing suitcase and a crying emoji. He didn't even bother to respond.

What if he's changed his mind and doesn't show up? I'm about five seconds away from pulling out my phone and sending Dane a furious message for even convincing me to do this stupid plan when I turn a corner, and the long British Airways check-in counter stretches out in front of me.

I spot Cash almost immediately. He's leaning against the counter, hands stuffed into a comfy-looking pair of olive green sweatpants, and he's got a bright pink travel pillow wrapped around his neck. The sight of him should fill me with relief, but it doesn't. A fierce scowl twists his usually handsome features. He looks like he'd rather be anywhere but here.

I pretend like I don't notice the way he stiffens as I approach. 'Morning, Cash.'

The only response I get is a sharp nod.

Well, *fine*. If he doesn't want to play nice, then I won't bother either. I resign myself to waiting for Penelope in silence when a blonde blur runs up to me and peppers me with air kisses.

'Oh. My. God. Bailey, is that you?' a high-pitched voice calls out.

'Hi, Lacey,' I manage to get out between her shrieks.

Lacey Lou (@*LaceyLouXo*) is a titan on the influencer scene. She has over a million followers and the power to make or break a brand with just one post. I wouldn't say we're friends, but we've met a few times at PR events, and she's always been nice and friendly to me. Standing to the side is her rugby player boyfriend, Danny. He occasionally shows up in her posts – usually the 'pranking my boyfriend' type ones.

I look around to see who else is here. I see two women who I vaguely recognise. Meera and Sara. They run the popular vlog, *Vanilla and Spice*, documenting their interracial and queer relationship to hundreds of thousands of fans on YouTube. I've never met them personally, but I've seen a few of their videos, and they seem adorable. They also get bonus points for the fantastic name 'Vanilla and Spice'.

Standing close by Meera and Sara is another face I recognise. Beatrice Rose, also known as *@ItsYourGirlBea*. I wouldn't call us rivals because I truly believe there's enough space for everyone to shine, but we do have a very similar audience base. She leans a little more toward high fashion than I do, but her hair tutorials are phenomenal and nearly always go viral. Today, she's got her hair in intricate straight-back cornrows, and she's wearing a colourful (and probably) designer tracksuit with a pair of Fendi slides. She's here with a man I don't recognise. She's definitely not posted him before.

Bea turns to look at me. I watch as her quizzical gaze slides from me to Cash and back to me again. Her lip twitches.

'I didn't know you were coming,' Lacey coos. 'I feel like I haven't seen you on my feed in forever. Where have you been?'

Hm. Has Lacey not seen The Video?

'And where's your man?' she asks, dramatically swivelling her head this way and that to peer through the crowd. She's searching for Ethan.

I glance up at Cash. He's glaring at a spot on the ground, but I don't have time to worry about him right now. He knew what he was signing up to.

'He's right here,' I say, pointing to Cash. To his credit, he looks up and offers Lacey a weak and brief smile. 'This is my boyfriend, Cash.'

Bea's perfectly plucked brows shoot into her hairline, and both Meera and Sara exchange a loaded look between them. Danny and Bea's so far unnamed boyfriend barely look up from their phones.

'Oh!' says Lacey, brows furrowing. It's clear that she was expecting to see Ethan. So she definitely hasn't seen The Video. That provides me with a little bit of comfort. Maybe it didn't go as viral as I thought it did.

'When did that hap—' Lacey begins, but she's interrupted by a smartly dressed woman approaching us. I take the opportunity to stand next to Cash.

'Sorry about that,' I mumble. He doesn't respond, and I don't even know why I bother.

'Hello, my lovelies!' the woman says brightly. 'I'm Penelope. It's lovely to meet you all in person. We don't have long before the flight, so let's get you all checked in now.'

As soon as she says that, Lacey, Meera and Bea all whip out their cameras, ready to start making content. I watch as Lacey sends Danny ahead of her in the line so she can get a clip of him walking towards the check-in counter.

I take my phone out tentatively. Should I be filming this too? I hate how I'm second-guessing myself. Where has my confidence gone? I decide against filming and stick my phone back in my pocket.

'You all right?' Cash murmurs to me as we shuffle forwards in the queue.

'You done ignoring me?' I ask. I know it's petty, but I'm already tired of the moody act. 'Listen, I know you don't want to be here with me. You're just in it for the holiday. I get it.'

We inch forward in the queue. Ahead of us, Bea is taking a photo of her and her boyfriend's passports.

'But you knew what you were getting into when you agreed to come,' I continue. 'If you're not going to play the part, tell me now. I'd rather cut my losses right here than have this all go to hell in Jamaica.'

He looks alarmed by my outburst, which brings me a sense of satisfaction. Did he really think I was going to spend the whole week letting him ignore me and treat me like dirt? Though, to be fair, he has been doing it all our lives, so why would I expect any different now?

'Sorry,' he mutters after a beat or two of stunned silence. 'I wasn't ignoring you.'

I scoff. 'All you do is ignore me, Cash. And you can get right back to it after the trip.'

'I told you, I'm not—'

'Save it, Cash,' I say abruptly. I'm in no mood to hear his excuses. 'I know you don't like me, and that's fine. But I just need this to go well.' I hate how needy and desperate I sound, but it's true. 'I need my life back.'

Cash looks like he wants to say something, but instead, he shakes his head. Wavy curls fall in front of his face, and again, I'm struck with the urge to run my fingers through them.

'Got it,' he says curtly. I know that he probably wants to say more. That there are probably insults on the tip of his tongue, but I'm impressed by his restraint.

After we check in, Penelope informs us that we've got about an hour until we need to be at our gate. She leads us over towards the British Airways lounge and tells us to relax and that she'll come and find us when we need to leave.

I want to dip into a booth and sit by myself, away from Cash and the others. But the rest of the group all stick together, so I begrudgingly join them at their table. Cash follows me without saying a word.

'Does everyone know each other?' Lacey asks once we've all settled into our comfy armchairs. I'm not sure why she's become the de facto leader of the group – maybe because she's got the most followers? – but it doesn't bother me. I'm happy to lean back in my seat and let her take the lead.

'I recognise everyone,' says Meera brightly. 'Even if we've not met in person before. Bea, I loved your Skims try-on haul last month. You made me run out and buy that dress in three different colours!'

'Thanks, girl,' Bea says with a bright smile. 'This is my boyfriend, Marcus, by the way.'

Marcus gives us all a wave.

'I didn't know you had a boyfriend,' says Lacey. 'You've kept that quiet.'

Bea laughs. 'I know, I know. I like to keep some things off the feed, you know? And Marcus isn't really the social media type.'

'Watch out, lad,' says Danny. 'I wasn't the social media type either, and now I'm in every video.'

'Bailey, it's so good to see you here,' says Sara. She's smiling sweetly, but I can't help but hear the unsaid '*What the hell are* you *doing here?*' instead.

My strained smile flickers. 'You too,' I say, hoping my voice doesn't sound too clipped. 'This should be a fun week.'

'Ooh, shall we get a group pic?' Lacey asks. She doesn't wait for a response before she whips out her phone and sticks out her arm. 'Come on, come on. Get around here. I think we should all fit.'

I glance at Cash and offer him a small shrug. *Sorry, Cash. Welcome to the influencer life.*

We all shuffle behind Lacey, who remains in her seat, and smile up at her camera. Cash is standing so close behind me that my back brushes up against his chest. I shiver at the contact and fight the urge to turn around and see if Cash is bothered by it at all.

'One, two, three!' Lacey snaps the photo and then quickly inspects it. 'Ew. No.' We take another six before we have one that she approves of. 'There. Posted!'

My phone vibrates with a notification from Instagram.

> @LaceyLouXo has mentioned you in their story

I tap it and immediately show Cash. Lacey's put a soft filter over the photo that makes all of our skin look vaguely golden. Cash and I are squashed in the corner, and I *think* we look like a real couple. I'm leaning into him, my back pressing up against his chest, and from the angle she's taken the photo, it looks like he's resting his chin on my head.

'Not bad,' Cash says, peeking over my shoulder.

I hum in agreement. 'I think I might share it. Are you okay with that?'

'Why wouldn't I be okay?' he asks.

'I'm just checking because your face is in it.'

'It's fine. I look pretty good.'

I roll my eyes, mostly because it's true. He looks amazing. But, then again, when does he not? I take a deep breath and prepare to reshare the photo to my own story. I add a small caption that says, '*Jamaica bound*!' and then hit share.

It's my first post since The Video went viral, and every single nerve in my body is on edge as I watch the story upload.

'You want a drink?' Cash says suddenly. 'You look really stressed.'

I snort. 'Understatement of the year.'

'Come on,' he says.

We make our way to the lounge bar. I order a cranberry and vodka, and Cash orders the same.

'I'm not a big drinker,' he says. 'So I'm trusting you.'

'It's my default drink,' I say, hopping up onto a bar stool. Cash doesn't sit down. Instead, he leans against the bar.

'You like berry flavours.'

It's not a question. More of an observation. A very astute observation.

'I do,' I say as I sip my drink. 'I'm surprised you noticed.'

Cash shrugs. 'I notice a lot of things.'

'Like what else?'

He opens his mouth like he's about to answer, then closes it and smirks. 'You'll have to find out.'

'That sounds like a challenge.'

Cash leans forward, entering my personal space. I freeze as his hair brushes against my cheek. He picks up his glass and pulls back, seemingly unaware of just how close we just were.

'Maybe it is,' he says as he sips his drink. 'This isn't too bad.'

'I'd never steer you wrong, Cash.'

'Hm, that remains to be seen. We've still got a week to go. Plenty of chances to steer me wrong.'

I clutch my chest and huff out an overly dramatic gasp. 'I'd *never*! Don't you trust me?'

'Of course I do.' And he sounds completely earnest.

'Well then, I'm going to need you to trust that I won't steer you wrong. This is about to be the best week of your life.'

He smiles that beautiful sunshine smile from the café, and I feel my heart stutter for a second.

'I'm gonna hold you to that.'

★ ★ ★

Cash and I sit near the back of the plane, far away from the others. Although we're closer to the toilet than I would have liked, not having to keep up the 'boyfriend-girlfriend' act for another ten hours is a blessing. I'm not sure how well it's going.

Penelope, Lacey and Danny all seem convinced, and I don't know Meera and Sara well enough to get a gauge on them. But Bea . . . Bea could be a problem. She's not said anything, but I've caught her staring at Cash and me curiously, and I know she's definitely got questions. Thankfully she's kind enough not to ask anything in front of the group, but I know that she's waiting for the perfect moment to strike.

Cash is definitely taking advantage of the distance between us and the others. The second we step away from the group, any pretence of liking me is gone. He doesn't even wait for me before he storms ahead to find our seats. It's getting a bit tiring dealing with this yo-yo personality of his.

By the time I reach our row, he's already slumped in the window seat, leaning against the window, eyes firmly squeezed shut.

The friendly and easy-going Cash I'd enjoyed a drink with in the lounge is gone. Asshole Cash is back. I don't know why it irks me, but it does. Just what is it about me that he dislikes so much?

I stow my carry-on in the overhead compartment and then drop down into the aisle seat. Cash doesn't stir, even as I jostle him as I get comfortable.

This is going to be a long week.

I whip out my phone as the flight attendants begin their cabin checks.

> **INSTAGRAM**
>
> **34 notifications**

I swallow as I tap on the icon and bring up the app. About thirty people have liked my last story post, and four of them have responded. Amber is right at the top of my DMs.

@amberrrr_ *HAVE FUN!! TAKE LOTS OF PICS. POST THEM.*

The other three responses are from people I don't know.

@leigh.dove34 *OOOH!! where is your jumper from? so cute!*

@blue_birdgal *so jealous, have fun!*

And the last message.

@gail23456862 *lol. is this one taken too?*

The last message makes my heart jump into my throat. I delete it without opening it, and it takes all my strength not to delete the entire story.

This is actually quite tame compared to the messages I got shortly after The Video went viral, but it's enough to have me doubting this whole plan.

I switch my phone to aeroplane mode and hope the ten hours will be enough to get me out of this mindset.

The plane begins to taxi, slowly picking up momentum as it rolls down the runway. I glance over at Cash. He's turned away from me as much as the small space will allow.

Seriously? What an *ass*. Does he think I'm going to give him a disease or something?

The plane makes a turn, and Cash squeezes his thighs. He's gripping them so tightly his hands have gone white, and I'd be willing to bet that there are tiny crescent marks in the fabric of his sweatpants.

The plane jerks slightly as we crawl over an uneven patch on the ground, and Cash inhales sharply.

I realise something that makes me feel awful.

Cash is a nervous flyer.

Suddenly his behaviour back in the airport makes sense. He was probably trying to psyche himself up to board the plane. A wave of sympathy washes over me, and before I can really give it much thought, I put my hand over his.

He stiffens slightly and cracks open an eye.

'Are you okay?' I ask.

He closes his eyes again. 'Mm. I just—' A deep, shuddery inhale. 'I hate take-off. Landing too. I'll be fine once we're in the air.'

'Do you need anything?'

'I'm fine,' he murmurs. He hasn't opened his eyes again, but I can feel the tension leaving his body as I squeeze his hand. 'I promise. Just give me ten minutes.'

'All right.'

I keep my hand over his, and he doesn't seem to mind. It doesn't feel as weird as it should. There's a warmth emanating from him that is oddly comforting. There are a few callouses, but his hand is surprisingly soft for someone who works in construction, and before I can help myself, I start to imagine his hands wandering down the length of my body.

I'm not sure where the thought comes from, but I picture his hands ghosting gently down my sides before dipping down past my belly button and slipping under—

'I think I'm good now.'

Cash's voice snaps me out of my impromptu fantasy, and I open my eyes. I hadn't even realised I'd closed them.

We're in the air now, and Cash looks noticeably less stressed.

'Thanks,' he says as he pulls his hand out from underneath mine.

'No problem,' I say. And I try not to think about how cold my hand suddenly feels.

★ ★ ★

The rest of the flight is uneventful. Cash spends most of it sleeping, and I'm left aimlessly scrolling through the in-flight movie selection. I end up watching all three *Magic Mike* movies and treat myself to six hours of Channing Tatum gyrating on stage.

Cash wakes up halfway through *Magic Mike XXL* and raises a brow once he notices what's on my screen. I give him a half-hearted smile, and, to his credit, he doesn't say anything. I wouldn't say he's been the chattiest person during the flight, but when the pilot's voice crackles through the speakers to tell the cabin crew to prepare for landing, Cash suddenly stiffens.

'It'll be okay,' I say gently.

'I know,' Cash says through gritted teeth. 'I know it's stupid.'

'It's not stupid. We can't help our fears.'

He gives me a sideways glance. 'What're you afraid of?'

'Sharks. Dane made me watch *Jaws* and *Deep Blue Sea* back to back when I was seven. I've been traumatised ever since.' I shudder as I remember the scene in *Deep Blue Sea* where Samuel L. Jackson gets eaten by a shark. It's haunted me for years and still makes me uneasy whenever I see a large body of water.

Cash snorts. 'I guess I'll be on shark watch this week.'

'Oh, I'm not getting in the sea,' I tell him. 'I'll paddle around in a pool, but not the sea. It makes me too nervous. And I can't swim.'

Before he can respond, we jerk forward as the plane hits a tiny bit of turbulence on its descent. Cash's face goes pale, and he grips the armrest so tightly that I'm afraid he's going to pull the leather off.

'Just focus on me,' I say softly as I reach out to hold his hand. As soon as our skin makes contact, Cash yanks his hand away.

The sting of his rejection hits me harder than I expect.

'Sorry,' I mumble. 'I was just trying to—'

Cash brings his hand back, entwines his fingers with mine and squeezes tightly.

'Like this,' he mutters. His eyes are shut, and his jaw is clenched tightly. 'If you don't mind.'

I look down at our hands, clasped together like two perfect puzzle pieces.

'I don't mind,' I say. And I don't. Not one bit.

Chapter Six

We wheel our suitcases into a wall of heat the second we leave the airport. It feels like the air is on fire. The sun beats down on us without relenting. There's a brightly coloured installation sign that reads WELCOME TO JAMAICA right outside the airport, and we all take turns posing in front of it.

While we're waiting for our turn in front of the sign, Cash sheds his sweatshirt. Underneath it, he's wearing a white string vest that leaves very little to the imagination. I sneak a glance at him and take in his subtle but impressive muscles. My gaze drops down to the defined *V* below his belly button and the trail of light, wavy hair that dips into the waistband of his sweatpants.

'Bailey, Cash, your turn!' Penelope yells. She grabs my phone out of my hand. 'Tell me what you want. Think of me as your personal photographer whenever you need me this week.'

She's a welcome distraction from my sudden ogling of Cash's admittedly attractive body.

'How do you want me?' Cash asks once we're in front of the sign.

It feels like a loaded question, and I swallow. I'm also acutely aware that the others are all watching. I catch Bea's eye briefly, and that quizzical look is still there.

We need to make this believable.

'Put your arm around my waist and smile,' I instruct.

He does what I say without any resistance and smoothly snakes his arm around my waist. His fingers ghost over the slightly exposed area of skin where my crop top ends, and I bite back the urge to shiver.

Penelope spends the next two minutes taking photos of us. She's obviously a pro. Without having to be prompted, she gets as many angles as humanly possible and shouts out helpful instructions like '*Cash, turn your head a teeeeeeny bit to the left. No, no, too much. Now, that's too little. Perfect!*'

Cash takes it all in his stride and commits to becoming mine and Penelope's puppet for the photos.

Once Penelope assures us that she's definitely got what she calls *The Money Shot*, I move to step away from Cash.

'Hold up,' Cash says. He keeps his grip on my waist. To my surprise, he pulls out his own phone, opens the camera app and taps the 'front camera' button. Our faces quickly fill his screen. 'Come on, smile.'

I do as he says, my lips splitting into an easy smile. Cash grins too, that beautiful sunshine smile again, and snaps the photo.

'You don't look half bad,' he smirks, finally pulling his arm away from me.

'Someone has to be the hot one in this relationship,' I throw back to him.

He blinks twice, then laughs. 'Fair.'

Penelope hands me back my phone, and I quickly scan through the photos she took. If I'm being honest, they're *brilliant*. Cash and I look every bit the loved-up couple ready to spend a romantic week in Jamaica together. But for some reason, I prefer the photo Cash took on his phone. Penelope's photos look staged, but we look natural in Cash's one. Like we've been together for years.

'Will you send me that?' I ask him as we follow the rest of the group towards the blissfully air-conditioned taxi waiting for us.

'You going to post it?' Cash raises a brow.

'Would you mind?'

Cash scratches at his jaw. He does that every so often when he's really thinking about his answer. 'I wouldn't.'

'Then, I think I will. I'll do a carousel grid post with some other photos thrown in.'

Cash gives me an easy shrug. 'You're the professional. I'm just here to do what you tell me to.'

It's a throwaway comment, and I know I shouldn't read into it, but I still feel bad about the way I snapped at him at the airport.

'I'm not your boss,' I mumble. 'This is your holiday too. You don't just have to do whatever I say.'

His lips curl up into a sly grin as he meets my gaze. 'Maybe I want to.'

If I didn't know any better, I'd say that Cash was flirting with me. But I do know better, so I brush off his playful tone with a roll of my eyes.

He doesn't like me, I remind myself as I climb into the large taxi waiting for us. He's just doing me a favour, nothing more.

Our resort is about an hour's drive from the airport. Penelope points out landmarks and interesting attractions as we drive past them, but I pay very little attention. I didn't sleep much on the flight, and it's starting to hit me. My eyelids feel heavy, and keeping my head upright is starting to hurt.

'Here.' Cash pulls his travel pillow off the strap of his carry-on and hands it to me. 'Use this. It's pretty comfy.'

'I'm fine,' I yawn. 'We'll be there soon.'

'Penelope says we've got another forty minutes.'

Forty minutes? I snatch the pillow from Cash and wrap it around my neck. I'm immediately hit with Cash's scent. I've never noticed it before, but now it floods my senses. I realise that it's unmistakably him. And I quite like it.

I lean back into the pillow and close my eyes. I'm out like a light within seconds, my hazy thoughts filled with images of Cash hovering over me, his lips twisted into a sultry smirk, his thigh pressed between my legs.

★ ★ ★

'We're here, Bailey.'

Cash gently jostles me awake after what feels like no time at all. When I open my eyes, the others have already climbed out of the taxi, and it's me and Cash left. His grey-green eyes crinkle with a hint of a smile as he watches me stretch and rub some of the sleep out of my eyes. I reach for my carry-on, but he easily grabs it and takes it with him as he climbs out of the taxi.

'Welcome to the You and I Couples Resort,' Penelope says with a wide grin once I've exited the taxi. 'Your little bit of paradise for the next week. We pride ourselves on creating the ultimate romantic experience for our couples, and we just know you're going to love your stay with us.'

The resort is stunning. I pull my phone out to take a video, and I'm not the only one. Lacey, Bea and Sara are all spinning around on the spot, making sure to get every angle possible.

We're standing in a large driveway in the middle of a sprawling green garden that stretches out into the distance. Large palm trees line the driveway leading up to an enormous white building with oak wood doors and windows. The large doors at the entrance are open, giving a sneak peek into the glamorous reception area where a row of smartly dressed men and women wait to greet us. I can see a sliver of white sand behind the hotel.

'This is the main entrance,' Penelope explains, walking us up the driveway. 'There are several apartments attached to this building here, but you'll each be staying in one of our private standalone suites at the south end of the resort. We only have five, and I promise you, they are the height of luxury. I know you all must be tired, so we don't have anything too strenuous planned for today. Go to your rooms, relax, explore the resort in your own time. And then we'll meet for dinner at The Blue Mahoe. We have three restaurants in the resort. The first two are open to all guests at any hour, and you don't require a booking. The Blue Mahoe is our Michelin-starred luxury restaurant headed up by Chef Bernard Pépin.'

'Oh, I love him!' Meera says suddenly. 'He did a pop-up in London last year, and it was *divine*.'

Penelope grins. 'Yes, you're all in for a treat. The Blue Mahoe is by reservation only, and we've booked it out just for you this evening. We've also got a candlelit meal on the beach just behind the restaurant planned for you all later in the week. But if you'd like to dine again outside of these two meals, please let me know, and I'll happily arrange that for you. After that, we've arranged for some local cocktails at the cabana bar by the pool.'

Everyone murmurs in excitement and anticipation for tonight, but I can't bring myself to join in. I'm still so damn tired.

'What time is dinner?' I ask, barely managing to conceal my yawn.

'7pm,' says Penelope. 'So you've got plenty of time to have a quick nap.' She throws me a wink.

'Is there a dress code for tonight?' Bea asks.

'It's a Michelin-starred restaurant,' Lacey says. 'Dress to impress.'

'Exactly,' says Penelope. 'Now, off you go. I'll see you this evening.'

I'm on autopilot as we follow the helpful porter to our suites. The resort is so big we have to take a golf cart to get to the south end. The check-in staff inform us that ours is close to Bea and Marcus's, so the four of us hop in the same golf cart. Cash and Marcus sit up front with the porter, peppering him with questions about the cart. I hear Cash asking if he can drive, but the porter shakes his head and mumbles something about insurance and liability.

It's hard to focus on them. Not only because I'm so tired but because Bea is staring me down. She's not subtle about it either. I don't know whether to be annoyed or impressed at how ballsy she is.

'I think I'm already starting to tan,' I say in an effort to be polite. 'Feels so good to be under the sun, right?'

'Sure,' says Bea, like she doesn't care at all. 'How long have you two been together?' She nods at Cash.

'Not long,' I say lightly, hoping I don't sound as nervous as I feel. I decide to bite the bullet. 'Obviously, you've heard about me and Ethan.'

'I think *everyone's* heard.'

'Not Lacey,' I say, as if that means anything.

Bea snorts. 'She's in her own one-million-follower world. She doesn't notice anything if she's not involved somehow.' She pauses and clears her throat. For the first time, she seems a little unsure of herself. 'You know, The Video was—'

Our golf cart grinds to a halt, and I'm spared from whatever it is she wants to say about The Video. I take advantage of the opportunity and hop out of the cart before she can say another word.

I have no doubt that The Video will likely become a topic of discussion at some point during the week; that is, if the girls haven't already gossiped about it together on the flight. But not yet. Let me enjoy some of the Jamaican sun before I'm forced to revisit my greatest shame.

We wave goodbye to Bea and Marcus as the golf cart continues on to their suite and then make our way inside. Cash grabs my big suitcase, leaving me with just my carry-on.

'I can get that,' I say, following him up the pathway. 'Seriously, you don't have to.'

'You're tired,' Cash says with a shrug. 'I've got it.'

I absolutely don't marvel at the way his muscles flex slightly as he pulls both mine and his suitcase up the pathway.

I clear my throat and rush ahead of him to open the door for him.

Penelope wasn't kidding when she called the standalone suites the height of luxury. The front door opens into a spacious foyer that's probably bigger than my bedroom back at my parents' house. I step further in, my mouth falling open in shock as I enter an *enormous* room with floor-to-ceiling windows and a sliding door that lines the entire back wall. Beyond the confines of our resort, I can see the expansive and beautifully blue Caribbean Sea and a colourful barrier reef. Just off the terrace, I can spy a large infinity pool that all the suites along this row must share.

Cash whistles as he enters the main room. He drops our suitcases to the floor and looks around. 'Damn.'

Damn is *right*. There's a giant canopy bed against one wall that's at least king-sized, a flat-screen TV on the other wall, and a comfortable-looking living area with a six-person couch in it. We peer into the bathroom. It's impeccably clean and shiny, and I marvel at the large walk-in shower, imagining how good it's going to feel washing off ten hours of travel in there.

'Hang on,' Cash says suddenly. 'There's just the one bed.'

I run back into the main room. I don't know why I bother to check because he's obviously right. There's only the one giant bed.

Cash laughs, but it's not his usual laugh. It sounds weird and almost a little choked. 'You'd think they'd be able to fit another bed in here.'

'We're supposed to be a couple,' I remind him, and I sound just as choked as he does. 'It makes sense that they'd give us a suite with only one bed.'

'I guess you're right.'

I glance at him, but he refuses to meet my gaze.

'I'll sleep on the couch,' he says. He walks over to it and plops down on it. 'It's big enough, and it's really comfy.'

'Don't be silly,' I say. I pad over to him and drop down next to him. He's right. It *is* ridiculously comfy. Like sitting on a cloud. 'You're doing me a favour by coming here. I'll take the couch. You take the bed.'

'What kind of gentleman would I be if I did that?'

I raise a brow. 'I didn't know you were a gentleman.'

He clutches at his chest and pretends to be offended. 'After I just carried your suitcase all the way here?'

'Oh yes, that incredibly long and arduous journey up the pathway.'

'I'm glad you agree.' He flashes that grin again, then drops his voice and leans in close. 'And you're taking the bed.'

It's a command. One that sends a shiver down my spine and makes my toes curl.

I force myself to meet his gaze. 'No.'

Something flashes in his eyes. Is it shock? Intrigue? I'm not sure. He shifts slightly on the couch, angling his body away from mine.

'*Bailey*,' he manages to get out, his voice a low, borderline growl. 'What else are we supposed to do?'

I lick my lips.

'We can share,' I manage to choke out. 'We can take a side each. The bed's big enough; I'm sure we can keep to our own sides.'

'Are you sure?' His voice is hoarse like it's been hours since he last had a drink.

'I'm sure.'

He gives me a jerky nod and then abruptly stands up. 'Do you mind if I shower first?'

He doesn't wait for my response before he grabs his carry-on and disappears into the bathroom. I wait until I can hear the sound of running water before I let out a deep breath.

There's something between us. A weird tension that I can't quite put my finger on. To take my mind off him, I pull out my phone and connect to the suite WiFi.

My phone immediately starts to vibrate with messages.

MUM
> Have you landed yet? Let me know as soon as you can x

AMBER
> Lemme know when you land

> Omg are you there yet? Flight tracker says yes but I need confirmation pls

I respond to them both quickly and let them know we've landed safely. I send Amber a quick video of the suite, and she immediately messages back.

AMBER
> Holy shit that is NICE

> Definitely post that video

> Also . . . am I going mad . . . or is there only ONE BED IN THAT ROOM?

Before I have the chance to message her back, her face fills my screen as she tries to video call me. Cash is still in the shower, but I don't want to risk him hearing me, so I slip out onto the terrace through the sliding doors.

'You look like you need a nap,' Amber says.

'I do.' I grimace. 'But I need to shower first. I'm waiting for him to finish in there.'

'How's it going? You know, the whole fake boyfriend thing?'

I tell her everything that's happened since we got to the airport back in London, and by the time I get to telling her about the bed, she's got a wide grin on her face.

'This is so hot,' she says bluntly. 'You're literally in a cheesy rom-com. You could be Sandra Bullock right now.'

'There's nothing hot about any of this,' I say. 'He's still the same old Cash. He's just doing me a favour.'

Amber hums and wiggles her brows. 'Why would a guy who supposedly loathes you agree to do this with you?'

She's got a point, but it's easily countered. 'He's Dane's best friend. He probably thinks of it like he's doing Dane a favour.'

Amber shakes her head just as a loud noise back in the suite catches my attention. I turn around. Cash is standing in front of the large window with a white towel slung low around his waist. I watch as he fumbles through his larger suitcase, looking for something.

His hair is dripping wet, and he keeps running a hand through it to push it back from his face. Apparently, he's found what he's looking for because he turns around with a look of triumph plastered across his face. I'm frozen to the spot as he looks up, and his eyes meet mine.

Amber is saying something, but I can barely hear her. My focus is entirely on Cash. I drink in every inch of him and commit his glistening body to memory.

I wonder what he's thinking as he slides open the door and pokes his head out.

'Shower's free,' he calls, and the smirk on his face is unmistakable. In this moment, I'm sure that he can read every single dirty thought that runs through my mind.

He disappears back inside, and Amber's voice finally cuts through the haze.

'You've gone so red. What happened?'

I exhale a deep, *deep* breath. I don't even know where to start.

Chapter Seven

'Stand a little bit to the left. Tilt your head a bit. Yeah, yeah, that's great.'

I've never been camera-shy. Mum loves to tell embarrassing stories about me as a child forcing my way to the front of any family pictures, and you can't really be an influencer if you don't like being in front of the camera. But, as I stand in front of Cash and let him snap photo after photo of me, I can't help but feel incredibly awkward.

We're about to head off to The Blue Mahoe for dinner. I've only ever really seen Cash in sweatpants and various Great Dane Construction Services T-shirts, so I'm very impressed with his holiday wardrobe so far. He's wearing a cream polo shirt with a pair of matching shorts. His outfit actually goes quite well with mine, a short, strappy blue corset dress that hugs my thighs.

'Move your hair a little bit,' he instructs.

I do as he says and flip my long curls over my shoulder. My dress is nice, but my hair is really the star of the show. I've decided I'm going to post a photo on the grid tonight and tag the brand. The thought has my stomach in knots, but Amber gave me a pep talk earlier, and I know I need to get it over and done with.

'I think we've got it,' he says. 'You want to check?'

'I trust you,' I say, taking my phone back. 'Shall we head out?'

I slip on my heels, and we open the door to find a golf cart waiting outside. The porter waves to us, and we hop in. It's only a two-minute drive to The Blue Mahoe, but it feels like an eternity. My bare thighs constantly brush up against Cash's, and every time our skin meets, I feel a shock buzz through me. I wonder if he feels it too.

When we get to the restaurant, the others are already there. We slide into the two empty seats next to Meera and Sara. As soon as we've sat down, Penelope claps her hands.

'Dinner will begin to be served shortly,' she says. 'Everything on the menu tonight has been locally sourced and features a delicious selection of fresh and flavourful dishes inspired by the many exotic flavours of the Caribbean Sea. Please take a look and enjoy.'

The menu is truly phenomenal. I don't know whether to choose the marinated lamb chops, supposedly 'grilled to perfection' and served with a tangy guava glaze, or the juicy and tender jerk chicken served with rice and peas and fried plantain.

After a minute or two of dithering, I opt for the jerk chicken – the promise of plantain too good to give up. Soon enough, waiters and waitresses begin to bring out our dishes. Lacey and Danny are sitting directly opposite us, and Bea and Marcus are to the left of them.

'I love your dress, Bailey,' says Bea. 'Such a nice colour on you. And your *hair*! Stunning!'

'Thanks,' I say, an easy grin spreading over my face. I take a lot of pride in my hair, and it always makes me feel good when someone notices. 'You look lovely too.'

As our dishes come out, the conversation around the table turns to our excitement about the next few days.

'We're definitely going to do the jet-skiing,' says Bea. 'That was Marcus's only requirement for coming on this trip.'

'Jet-skiing and some good rum,' laughs Marcus.

I watch them closely as we dig into our meals. You can tell they've been together for a while. There's something easy about the way they interact with each other. Marcus doesn't even need to ask before he slips a pile of mushrooms onto Bea's plate, and Bea doesn't even glance his way as she picks up his glass and gives his drink an experimental sip.

The others are the same. Meera and Sara have angled their chairs, so they're leaning into each other. I watch as they pick from each other's plates and do a cheesy arm loop to drink their wine. Danny's got an arm draped over Lacey's shoulders, and he seems to have no issue eating one-handed if it means he can maintain contact with her.

Bea is staring at Cash and me intently. I wonder what she sees when she looks at us. I glance over at him, and I'm surprised to see he's looking at me. Or to be accurate, he's looking at my plate.

'See something you like?'

His gaze flickers back up to me and lingers for just a beat too long. Despite the humid heat around us, I shiver.

'Are those plantain?' He points at the small pile on my plate. 'I've never had one before.'

I nod and pluck a piece from my plate. 'Feel free to try some. They're delicious. And it's plan*tain*. Like mountain.'

'Plan*tain*,' he says, with a teasing grin. 'Like abstain.'

I wonder if I'm imagining the way his eyes drop to my mouth as I pop the piece in. 'We're in Jamaica,' I tell him. 'You've got to say it like they do.'

He shrugs and, after a brief moment of hesitation, snatches one from my plate. He takes a tentative bite, then his eyes go wide, and he quickly devours the whole piece. 'That was great.'

I laugh. 'Welcome to your newest obsession. Dane and I could get through five fingers in a day when we were younger. Used to drive Mum mad.' I pick up another piece and squeeze it between my fingers. 'These are a little fatter than I usually have them. I like them crispier, and you generally have to slice them a bit thinner to get that.'

'I'll have to try some of yours when we get back home.'

I shrug. 'Sure.'

It occurs to me that, aside from our staged photo outside the airport, this is the most couple-like we've been since the trip began. I wonder if we're doing a good job.

'Do you want some of mine?' He doesn't wait for me to answer before he cuts off a piece of lamb and spears it with the tip of his fork. He waves the fork around a little and grins. 'Try it.'

I hesitate, then remember how casually the others are all eating off each other's plates. I lean over and bite the piece of lamb clean off his fork. The lamb, cooked to perfection, melts in my mouth and I can't help but close my eyes and hum in appreciation as I chew. 'That's amazing.'

When I look over at Cash again, his eyes are wide and focused on me. His tongue darts out to run over his lips. 'Glad to hear it.' His voice sounds gruff, choked even, and he quickly turns away from me and pokes at his own plate.

'So, Ethan,' Lacey says suddenly. 'What do you do?'

I stiffen in my seat.

The quiet hum of conversation around the table stops in an instant. Lacey's cheeks start to redden as she realises what she's said.

'Sorry, sorry, sorry! My bad,' Lacey grimaces, and to her

credit, she does actually look apologetic. 'Sorry, it just slipped out. I'm so used to seeing Bailey and Ethan on my feed.' She turns to me, her expression shifting from apologetic to inquisitive. 'Girl, what happened?'

Everyone is staring at me. I knew that this would come up eventually, but I can't believe she's asking in front of everyone. My breathing gets heavier, and my heartbeat quickens.

'I don't think Bailey wants to talk about that.' Cash's voice is polite enough, but there's a coldness to it that leaves no room for argument.

'Shit,' says Lacey. 'Of course. Bailey, I'm—'

I don't wait to hear her apology. I push my chair back, mumble something about needing the bathroom, and run.

★ ★ ★

Ethan WAS a dickhead who cheated on me for the entirety of our relationship. Even before I found out about the cheating, he used to treat me like he was some kind of prize, and I should feel lucky to be with someone like him. I know that I shouldn't be wasting tears over someone like him. And yet here I am, dabbing away tears in *Jamaica*, of all places. I'm angry at Lacey for embarrassing me in front of everyone and furious at myself for being so weak.

'Bailey?'

The door to the bathroom opens to reveal Bea, Meera

and Sara. They stand there for a second or two, taking in my red eyes and tear-stained cheeks, before all three of them spring into action.

'Oh, God, *Bailey*,' Sara whimpers, hurrying into the bathroom. Before I can say anything, she's pulled me into a hug like we're lifelong friends and didn't just meet a few hours ago. 'Are you okay?'

'I'm fine,' I say, my voice noticeably clipped.

Bea rolls her eyes. 'You don't have to lie to us, you know? Here.' She reaches into her purse and hands me some blotting paper. 'Just dab it on your cheeks. That way, you won't ruin your make-up.'

'I think we're wearing the same blush,' says Meera, rifling through her own purse. 'Fenty "Cheeks Out"? Here, you can top up with some of mine.'

Sara pulls away from me so I can wipe away my tears and reapply my blush.

'Thanks,' I say once I'm finished. 'You guys didn't have to do this.'

'We have to stick together,' says Meera earnestly. 'That wasn't cool back there. I don't know what Lacey was thinking.'

'She wasn't thinking,' says Bea with another roll of the eyes. 'You know how she is. I'm not excusing her or anything, but I doubt she meant it maliciously.'

'Yeah,' says Sara. 'I think she was just surprised, that's all. We all were, if I'm being honest.'

I take a deep breath. 'I know. I'm guessing you all saw—'

'Yeah,' says Sara. She drops her gaze for a moment. 'We all saw The Video.'

'I—' I begin, but Bea cuts me off.

'Listen, whatever happened between you and Ethan, that's your business. It sucks that it got made public like that, but you don't need to explain anything to us. Especially if you're not ready to.'

A wave of gratitude washes over me.

'Thank you.'

'And who cares about Ethan?' says Meera. 'Not gonna lie, Bailey. Cash is *definitely* an upgrade there.'

Everyone shoots her a look.

'What?' Meera laughs. 'Just because I'm gay doesn't mean I can't tell whether a man's good-looking or not.'

That gets a laugh out of everyone, and I feel some of the tension I'm carrying start to float away.

'I was half expecting you to introduce him as just a good friend,' Sara says. 'How long have you guys been dating? You seem so new.' She interprets the look of panic on my face as something else and quickly starts to backtrack with a nervous laugh. 'I mean, *obviously*, you guys are new. I just mean—'

'It's fine,' I say quickly. I offer her a small smile to try and quell her obvious nerves. 'I know what you mean, and it's fine. We've been together for about a month now,' I shrug. 'New relationship nerves and all that. We're seeing how things are going.'

Meera and Sara look happy enough with that explanation, but I can tell Bea's not convinced. I don't know what I'll do if it gets out that I've faked a relationship with Cash in order to get a free trip to Jamaica. I don't think I'll be able to handle the embarrassment. Between this and The Video, I think it will spell the end of my career entirely.

'Let's get back out there,' I say quickly before Bea can add anything else.

Meera pulls her phone out of her purse. 'Before we go, let's take a photo.'

We all squish in front of the mirror and pose. It's a cute moment, and I'm filled with a sudden sense of camaraderie. Amber is the closest thing I have to a sister, but in this moment, it feels like I have another three.

'Come on,' says Bea. 'Penelope said they'll probably be at the cabana bar for cocktails. Let's go.'

We step out into the hall, and I'm suddenly face-to-face with Cash. He's leaning against the wall opposite the bathroom door, and there's a thunderous expression pasted across his face. The second we make eye contact, his features smooth slightly, but a cloud of anger and irritation still lingers.

'We'll meet you two at the bar,' Bea says. Meera and Sara both echo her, and the three quickly disappear down the hall. Once they're no longer in sight, Cash steps towards me.

I don't know why, but I'm holding my breath. I've never seen him look so mad before. Is he mad at *me*? Did I embarrass him too?

He closes the gap between us and, to my surprise, envelops me in a gentle hug. He gives me a squeeze, then pulls back and looks directly into my eyes.

'Are you all right?' he asks, voice low.

I blink up at him. That's not what I was expecting him to do or say. I can still feel the phantom warmth of his arms around me. 'I'm fine.'

'You sure? We don't have to go back out there. We can head back to the suite.'

'No,' I say. It's a tempting offer, but I don't want to look like I'm running away any more than I already have. 'Thanks for coming to check on me, but I'm all good. She just . . . Lacey doesn't think things through all the time.'

'Yeah.' Cash's lips twist into a displeased frown. 'I can see that.'

'But it's fine,' I continue. 'She didn't mean any harm. Let's go to the bar and try and salvage the night.' I move to walk away, but Cash reaches out, grabs my hand and pulls me back towards him.

'Are you sure?' he asks me again. 'We don't have to stay anywhere that's going to make you feel like that.'

His voice is dripping with sincerity, like he truly does care about me. It's enough to make my heart stutter. But then I remember, he's just playing a role. None of this is real. I'm sure if I wasn't Dane's sister, he'd still be at the table enjoying his meal.

'I'm sure,' I say, my tone slightly clipped.

He holds my gaze for a few long seconds like he's searching for something in my eyes. Whatever it is he's looking for, he seems to find it because he drops my gaze and my hand and gives me a small shrug. 'Let's go then.'

As we walk to the bar, I remember what Sara said, and I groan.

Cash quirks a brow. 'What?'

'I don't think we're a very convincing couple. The girls told me they were expecting me to introduce you as just a good friend.' I glance at him sideways and then say, 'I think we're going to have to step our game up.'

His Adam's apple bobs up and down as he swallows. 'How do you mean?'

I shrug. 'Be a bit more touchy-feely, I guess? Act like we're actually into each other.' That's rapidly becoming a non-problem for me, but I push those thoughts aside. 'You think you can do that?'

'I think I can manage,' Cash says slowly. A heady expression flashes across his features. 'You ready?'

I give him a nod, and we step out into the pool area where the cabana bar is located. There's loud music playing, and the others are already dotted around the bar on comfortable-looking chairs. Lacey looks up at me as we walk towards them, but I avoid her entirely. I don't need to be bombarded with a thousand apologies right now.

'You grab a seat,' I say, nodding to an empty pair of chairs by Bea and Marcus. 'I'll get us something to drink. Any requests?'

Cash shakes his head. 'I told you, I'm not a big drinker. I'll have whatever you have.'

I play it safe and order myself a porn star martini and a cranberry and vodka for Cash, since I know that he liked it back at the airport. While I wait for the bartender to mix our drinks, I watch Cash out of the corner of my eye. He's in the middle of a conversation with Marcus. He laughs at something Marcus says, and I find myself mesmerised by how relaxed he looks. Like he's genuinely enjoying Marcus's company.

A pang of jealousy hits me.

Cash's unnecessary dislike of me has never *really* bothered me. Until now. I've always just kind of brushed it off as a weird quirk of his and have never really taken it too seriously. Not everyone has to like me, and who wants to be friends with an egotistical ass like Cash Reid anyway, right? But as I watch him interact with the others – they're all crowding around him now, like moths to a flame – I realise that I don't know Cash. Not the real Cash. And why does that bother me so much?

I realise that *I* want to be on the receiving end of one of Cash's genuine laughs. I want to be the reason he's throwing his head back, shoulders shaking, as a roar of laughter rips through his body.

I know that he's only here as a favour to Dane and to get a free holiday out of this and that the second we land back in London, things will go back to how they've always been between us. And the thought of that makes me sad.

As I walk back to him, I decide things are going to change. By the end of this trip, Cash and I are going to be friends.

Chapter Eight

I walk back to the group and place our drinks on the small glass table in front of Cash. He's in the middle of a heated conversation with Marcus and Sara about a TV show called *The Traitors*. I've never heard of it before, but Cash is wildly animated as he talks about it. It's oddly endearing to see, and I make a mental note to check out the show once we're back home.

I move to sit down in the empty seat next to Cash, but before I drop into it, something snakes around my waist.

It's Cash's arm.

Without interrupting his conversation or even breaking eye contact with the others, Cash deftly pulls me onto his lap. I jerk forwards instinctively to move away, but his grip on my waist tightens, holding me firmly in place.

What is he doing?

A rapid warmth spreads across my body as Cash guides

me until my back is flush against his chest. He leans forward suddenly to reach for his drink with his free hand, lips brushing against my ear as he moves back and forth.

'Is this okay?' he whispers.

I give him a jerky and hopefully imperceptible nod. I realise that this is his way of making our relationship seem believable. While I appreciate it, a heads-up would have been nice.

I grab my own drink, and when I lean back, his hand drops from my waist to rest on my exposed thighs. My breath catches in my throat as his fingers start tracing lazy patterns on my skin. Images of me lying on that giant bed in our room while Cash slowly runs his hands along every inch of my body flash through my mind at lightning speed.

Cash sips from his glass casually, completely unaware that he's ignited a fire within me. I glance around the pool area. If anyone is surprised by Cash pulling me onto his lap, they don't show it. Lacey and Danny are curled up in a dark corner together, but the others are still sitting by us. Marcus has unearthed an old pack of playing cards, and he's dealing them out to everyone so we can play a game of blackjack.

'You in, Bailey?' Marcus asks.

'Sure,' I say. I try and shimmy off Cash's lap, but he squeezes my thigh to stop me. I roll my eyes and glance over my shoulder. 'You'll see my cards.'

'I won't look.'

'That's exactly what a cheater would say.'

Cash looks at me. 'I don't cheat.'

I swallow. There's something in his tone that makes me think he's not only talking about the game.

Before I can respond, Cash shifts so he can lean forward and avoid looking at my cards. The movement sends me dipping down a bit, and the base of my spine brushes up against something hard.

I inhale sharply. Pressed up against me is Cash's rock-hard *dick*. I wiggle against him experimentally and grin as his dick twitches against me. A smug sense of satisfaction surges through me as I realise something.

Cash may not *like* me, but he's definitely *attracted* to me.

And I can work with that.

He grips my thigh a little tighter, and I can almost hear his silent warning. *Please stop.*

I don't.

Something feral comes over me, and I give him another wiggle, arching my back slightly as I pretend to look through my cards like I've actually got any skin in this game. The only thing I care about right now is Cash and the way his body feels beneath mine.

'*Bailey*,' he groans quietly in my ear, leaning forward to drop a card onto the table. '*Stop.*'

'Hm?' I hum innocently, my eyes wide with faux confusion. 'What's wrong?'

Something flashes in his eyes, and, this time, I recognise what it is. It's pure, unbridled arousal. And I'm sure it mirrors what he sees in my eyes.

'Are you cold?' he says suddenly and loudly.

Huh? Cold? We're in Jamaica, and I'm hotter than I've ever been, but Cash doesn't wait for me to respond.

'Meera, can you pass me that blanket behind you?' he calls. I wonder if I'm the only one who notices how choked he suddenly sounds. 'Bailey's getting a little cold.'

'Sure!'

Meera hands Cash a blanket from the pile hidden behind one of the chairs. He murmurs a *thanks* and then drapes the blanket over my lower half. As soon as I'm covered, his hand dips under the hem of my dress. I swallow down a quiet moan as he travels up my thigh. I try and stay as focused on the game of blackjack as I can, but Cash makes it incredibly difficult. My vision blurs slightly as his fingers reach the elastic of my panties. It's like I'm running on autopilot as I angle my hips downwards slightly, trying to coax his hand exactly where I need it to be.

'Bailey, your turn.'

I blink. They're already back to me? I throw down a random card and impatiently wiggle on Cash's lap. He's playing one-handed and easily keeping up conversation with the others while his other hand pulls down my panties and gives me one quick stroke.

My whole body stiffens, and I have to take a huge gulp of my cocktail to stop myself from crying out. I see stars in my eyes as Cash continues to lazily move his fingers up and down. His touch is somehow gentle and urgent at the same time.

I don't think I've ever been more turned on in my life.

'Are you all right, Bailey?'

I snap back to reality for a moment. Sara is looking at me with concern.

'Your face is really red. Are you okay?'

'Yeah,' I say, cringing at just how high my voice sounds. 'I'm fine. It's the alcohol. Always makes me go red.'

Sara gives me an understanding nod and then turns her attention back to the game.

'You're being too obvious,' Cash murmurs in my ear as he dips two fingers inside me. 'Relax.'

I squeeze my thighs together as pleasure shoots through my body. 'Not my fault,' I manage to pant out.

I can't believe we're doing this. In front of everyone. His dick twitches against me again, and I picture it straining against his shorts to break free. He's just as turned on as I am, and I know he wants to be inside me.

I press down onto him as much as I can, taking pleasure in the way he exhales deeply through his nostrils. In response, he presses his thumb against my clit, and I swear everything goes blurry for a good five seconds. I'm so close. And he knows it.

He quickens his rhythm, his fingers moving in and out of me with equal amounts of care and speed. He doesn't seem to mind as I slowly start to rock back and forth. I don't care if anyone else notices. I'll deal with that later. Right now, all I need is this sweet release and to return the favour somehow.

There. Right there.

My breathing quickens, my vision blurs, and—

Cash pulls his hand away and places it back on my thigh.

He leans forward to whisper in my ear, and I can *feel* the smirk tugging at his lips. 'I told you to stop.'

I blink, unsure of what to say. *What the fuck just happened?*

* * *

We hang by the bar and pool for another thirty minutes or so before the jet lag seems to hit us all at once, and we agree to call it a night. I can't say that bothers me.

I'm desperate to be alone with Cash. The air between us is thick with tension. We need to talk about what just happened, and I desperately need to get some kind of resolve.

Irritatingly, Bea and Marcus climb into a golf cart with us, prolonging the time it takes for it to just be me and Cash alone. Luckily, I'm able to mask my frustration as tiredness, and they don't question my moody silence as we approach our suites.

'See you tomorrow,' Bea and Marcus say as we hop out

of the golf cart and walk up the path to our suite. 'Maybe we can all meet and grab breakfast before we disappear for the day?'

'Sounds great,' says Cash. He grabs my hand and guides me up the pathway. 'Have a good night.'

I barely get out my own *goodnight* to them. I'm too transfixed by his hand. I remember where it was just half an hour ago, and I want it back there again.

As soon as we're inside the suite, Cash drops my hand and turns to face me. For some reason, he looks guilty.

'Bailey,' he starts, but then his phone vibrates angrily in his pocket. He pulls it out. 'Shit. It's my mum. I forgot to call her when we landed.'

'No, that's fine,' I say. 'Answer her. I'll get ready for bed.'

He still looks weirdly guilty, but he gives me a nod and then disappears outside onto the terrace. Before he slides the door closed behind him, I catch the beginning of their conversation.

'Hi, Mum. Yeah, we landed fine. Sorry. Yeah. Yeah. Yeah, she's great. No, I have—'

I want to hear more, but I give him the privacy he deserves. Instead, I quickly rush around and get ready for bed. When he comes back inside, I'm lying underneath the thin blanket with my hair wrapped for bed.

'Everything all right?' I ask as he slides the terrace door shut and makes sure that it's locked.

'Yep.'

I frown. His voice sounds clipped, and he's desperately avoiding making eye contact with me. 'Are you sure?'

'Mhm. I'm gonna get ready for bed.'

He grabs a few things from his suitcase and then disappears into the bathroom. When he comes out again, he's only wearing boxer shorts, and he's pulled his hair into a messy bun. It's an incredibly attractive look. I try my best not to ogle him as he walks over to the bed, but I'm not sure I succeed.

I expect him to drop right next to me in bed, but he doesn't. Instead, he climbs in at the very furthest end and makes himself cosy down there.

'Do you know what we're doing tomorrow?' he asks as if I'm not seconds away from jumping his bones.

'A waterfall hike,' I say. I stretch out an arm and swipe it across the empty space between us. 'Are you all right down there? You're so . . . you're so far away.'

'Isn't that what we agreed?' he asks, brows knitting in apparent confusion. 'You take one side; I take the other.'

I nod slowly. That *is* what we agreed, but I'd assumed, given everything that just happened by the bar, things would be different.

He pulls the blanket over himself and then glances over at me. 'You ready to turn the lights off?'

What? Are we just going to lie here and pretend nothing

has happened between us? Pretend like I didn't spend the latter half of the evening grinding on him, or like he didn't just bring me to the brink of orgasm in front of everyone?

When I don't answer, Cash turns away from me and hits the light switch on his side of the bed. The room is quickly plunged into darkness.

'Goodnight, Bailey.'

I don't respond. Instead, I lay there, staring up at the ceiling as Cash's breathing quickly evens out, and he falls asleep. Only one word comes to mind.

Fuck.

Chapter Nine

When I wake up, Cash is gone. The realisation fills me with relief.

I don't know what the hell happened between us last night, but I'm not happy.

I feel used.

I feel gross.

I feel *incredibly* horny.

I need some time to myself. I use my time alone in the suite to take some more videos and photos. Then I open Instagram and post one of my stories, remembering to tag the resort, and decide to finally post on the grid too. My last post is from four months ago now, and that familiar feeling of anxiety bubbles up inside me again as I scroll through my gallery, looking for the best photos to post.

Amber has suggested turning off comments completely. That way, I won't have to worry about the trolls, but that feels like I'm admitting defeat. And anyway, nobody turns off comments unless they have something to hide. Which I do, but still. The trolls don't need to know that.

I end up choosing one of the photos Cash took of me last night in my blue dress, along with a handful of photos and videos that showcase the beautiful resort and the delicious meal we had last night. I deliberate posting the photo Cash took of us on his phone outside the airport, but then I decide against it. I don't know what's happened between us, and I'm still angry over how he completely ignored me last night.

I hit *post* and then disconnect my phone from the WiFi. I promise myself I won't reconnect until this evening in an attempt to try and calm my anxiety.

By the time I've showered and gotten dressed, Cash still hasn't returned. A small part of me wants to reconnect to the WiFi and message him, but the petty and irritated part of me wins, and I pretend like his sudden absence doesn't bother me at all.

I head down to the restaurant closest to our villa – only a five-minute walk – and spot Bea, Meera, Sara and Lacey sitting around a table together. Meera waves me over with a bright smile on her face.

'Morning, Bailey! We've been messaging you for the last twenty minutes.'

'Sorry,' I say, sliding into the seat furthest away from Lacey, who is still staring at me with big, apologetic eyes. 'I disconnected from the WiFi for a bit.'

Meera nods sagely. 'A digital detox. Fair.'

'Where're the guys?' I ask.

'At the gym,' says Bea. 'Isn't Cash with them?'

I feel my jaw tighten at the mention of Cash, but I try and smooth my expression into an easy smile. I don't need them thinking that our relationship – however fake it is – has fallen apart on the very first night. 'That's right. I thought they'd be done by now.'

'Danny could spend all day in the gym,' Lacey pipes up. 'We'll probably have to go and grab them after breakfast.'

I shrug. 'Cash is a big boy. I'm sure he'll find his way back eventually.'

Will he continue to pretend like nothing happened between us last night, though?

I order a plate of eggs, bacon and toast for breakfast and fall into an easy conversation with the girls.

'What're you doing today?' I ask. We've all been sent Penelope's packed itinerary, but, for the most part, we can pick and choose which activities and excursions we'd like to do.

'We're doing a guided heritage tour,' says Sara. 'I think we're being driven to a town about an hour or so away from the resort, and we'll spend the day there lapping up the culture.'

'And eating good food,' adds Meera.

Sara nods. 'The tour is run by a local family, and they've invited us to have lunch with them too.'

'That sounds great,' I say. 'What about you, Bea? What're you and Marcus up to today?'

'Snorkelling,' Bea says. 'We're going to head down to the reef and spend the day there. Should be great.'

I nod. 'That sounds amazing. And you, Lacey?'

She looks surprised that I've asked her. 'We're going for a waterfall hike. It wasn't my first choice. I wanted to check out the beach, but Danny really wanted to give it a go, so . . .' She shrugs.

I resist the urge to grimace and hope I manage to school my expression into something more smile-like. 'We're doing the waterfall hike too.'

I picked the hike excursion specifically because Penelope promised that the hike wouldn't be too strenuous and that it culminates with a beautiful blue lagoon. Penelope actually called it *'the perfect romantic hideaway'*, which probably would have sold me on the excursion if our relationship were real. When she first mentioned it, I imagined taking a flurry of photos and videos of Cash and me playing up the dutiful loved-up couple role in the lagoon.

My excitement for the excursion has since dwindled significantly.

I don't particularly want to spend the day traipsing through the jungle with Lacey, and cuddling up with Cash in somewhere dubbed '*the perfect romantic hideaway*' is not at the top of my wish list right now. But it's too late to change my mind. The excursion has been booked, and we're due to head off in an hour or so.

'Ooh, *fun*,' Lacey says. 'It'll be just like a double date! You know, I didn't get the chance to apologise last night, but—'

I hold a hand up to stop her. I don't want to relive last night again. 'It's fine, Lacey. Let's just forget it ever happened.'

Lacey's smile is full of relief. 'Got it.'

After breakfast, I head back to the suite quickly to grab some comfortable trainers for the hike. As soon as I step into the suite, the bathroom door opens, and Cash comes sauntering out. I hate the way my throat goes dry as I take in his still-glistening body and the towel wrapped low around his waist. He doesn't deserve my attraction.

'Oh,' he says, blinking down at me. 'Morning, Bailey.'

'Good morning,' I say curtly as I storm past him with barely a glance. 'We're due at the front desk in ten minutes to leave for the hike.' I rifle through my suitcase and pick out my most comfortable pair of trainers hidden amongst a sea of strappy sandals and heels. 'I'll see you down there.'

'Bailey, wait.'

He moves to grab my arm as I brush past him, but I shake him off.

'*What?*' I spit, whirling around to face him. Even I'm surprised by the amount of venom I can hear in my voice. 'What do you want, Cash?'

'Last night—'

'Last night, you were just doing what I asked you to, and things got out of hand,' I say through gritted teeth. 'I get it. It didn't mean anything. Don't worry. I won't make that mistake again.'

Maybe if I say it enough times, I'll believe it too.

'*Bailey.*'

But I don't listen. I whirl around and storm out of our suite before he can spot the tears that quickly begin to well in my eyes.

★ ★ ★

A car takes us on a twenty-minute drive away from the hotel to the outskirts of the jungle. We're accompanied by a tour guide named Leroy, who happily informs us of all the names and uses of the exotic-looking plants we pass by. It's all incredibly interesting information, but I barely hear any of it.

Focusing on *not* looking focused on Cash is taking all my attention. I can see him out of the corner of my eye, desperately trying to catch my gaze, but I stare steadfastly ahead. I won't let him have the satisfaction of seeing how much his actions have affected me.

I pull out my phone and record the short drive through the window, getting shots of the winding roads and the clear ocean peeking out from over the side of the mountains we're crawling along.

The prospect of spending the day with Lacey and Danny hadn't filled me with excitement, but now I'm grateful for their presence. They're a convenient buffer between Cash and me. I don't even mind when Lacey monopolises the entire twenty-minute drive, bragging about her last PR trip to Dubai.

'Now, that was a *real* luxury trip,' Lacey says. 'Not that this isn't nice, because it is. Just that Dubai was on a whole other level, you know?'

'Sure,' I say, though I don't. I once went on a weekend trip to Cornwall with a cosmetics company which was fun enough, but this is definitely the biggest PR trip I've ever been invited on. It annoys me even more that Cash is here to experience this milestone in my career.

I'm starting to wish I'd chosen to bring anyone else. Surely even plucking a random man off Tinder would've been better than this?

'What about you, Cash?' Lacey swivels around in her seat to face him. 'Have you been anywhere nice recently?'

'Does Hastings count?' Cash jokes.

Lacey blinks at him. I'm not too sure she even knows where Hastings is.

'No,' Cash says eventually, once he realises he's not going to get a response from her. 'I don't really like flying. This is the first time I've stepped on a plane since I was a kid.'

My brows knit into a frown. I didn't know that. The question spills from my lips before I can catch myself. 'How come?'

Cash glances at me and quirks a brow as if to say, '*Oh, you've remembered I exist?*'

I raise my own brow in retaliation.

'Planes make me nervous,' he says with a shrug. 'Too many unknowns. I like to be in control or at least be able to see the person who is in control. I'd rather sit on a boat for twenty-four hours than get on a plane.'

I think back to the flight and remember how standoffish and nervous he'd been. I hadn't realised just how much he hated flying.

'Aw.' Lacey shoots us a sickly sweet smile. 'And he still agreed to come on this trip. Bailey, that's a keeper right there.'

And the thing is, she's right. Knowing that Cash was happy to get on a plane for me, despite his fears, makes my heart swell.

But then I remember last night and how he behaved in the aftermath of it all, and my expression clouds with irritation once more.

'We'll see about that,' I say.

Next to me, I feel Cash twitch, but he doesn't say anything.

Our car stops in a small clearing, and Leroy instructs us to get out.

'We'll start our hike here,' he says, his bald head shining in the relentless sun. 'It's about a twenty-minute walk to the waterfall. And we'll spend the afternoon there. Keep up, drink plenty of water, and let's go!'

Leroy leads us into the bushes, and we soon come across a small but well-worn pathway. Lacey and Danny storm ahead. Lacey's eager to get to the waterfall, and Danny seems happy enough to follow her. He's a bit like a puppy.

I purposely stay close to Leroy, asking him questions about the route we're taking and all the various plants and bugs we come across. Cash isn't far behind me, but he seems to respect that I'm in no mood to speak to him and doesn't make any effort to try and interrupt.

'This right here.' Leroy stops suddenly and points at a yellow bundle of vines. They're so thin they almost look like thread. 'This is called *dodder vine*. Any idea what it's used for?'

I shake my head. It doesn't look like anything special.

'It supposedly has some medicinal qualities,' Leroy explains. 'If you boil it with ginger, it can help to fight a chest infection. But that's not why it's so popular. It's got another name. Some people call it the *love bush*.' He grins, clearly impressed with himself for sharing the fact. If Cash and I were actually a couple, it might've been cute.

I give Leroy a polite smile and signal for him to continue.

'You take a bit of the vine and throw it on a different and fresh plant. If the vine continues to grow, then it means that love is on the horizon for you, but if not . . . well, maybe it's time to start looking elsewhere, hm?' He chuckles to himself and then continues on down the pathway.

As I pass the mangle of vines, I reach out and grab a handful. It comes apart from the rest of the bush with surprising ease. I place it on top of a nearby plant and imagine that it suddenly springs to life, signalling love on the horizon for me.

Cash steps beside me, casting a dark shadow over the bush. 'You believe that superstition?'

I jump, dropping the vines. I'd momentarily forgotten that he was still there. 'No. I just wanted to feel.'

Cash nods. His gaze flickers down the pathway. Leroy has turned a corner, and there's no sight of him now. 'Listen, Bailey. Can we talk?'

'There's nothing to talk about,' I say. I move to turn away, but Cash reaches out and grabs my hand. 'Let me go.'

'Can you just listen?' Cash asks, his voice pleading.

I wrench my hand out of his grip and stare up at him. 'What?'

'I just wanted—' He groans and runs a hand down his face. When he looks at me again, his eyes are wide and apologetic. 'I got carried away last night. We both did. I'm sorry.'

Irritation courses through me. Why is he rubbing this in? 'We've already covered this. And you don't have to be *sorry*. What's there to be sorry for? I liked it. And I thought you did too.'

'I did – I – *Bailey*,' he groans again and then shakes his head. 'You're my best friend's little sister.'

I roll my eyes. 'What does that have to do with anything?'

'There are some lines you just don't cross.'

'And fingering me in front of people isn't crossing that line?'

I think my bluntness disarms him because he drops his gaze. 'It is. And I'm sorry.'

I shake my head and turn away from him. 'I don't understand you, Cash. One minute you hate me. The next, you're touching me like we've been together for years. I don't know what game you're playing—'

'I'm not playing any games.'

'But it needs to *stop*. Figure out what you want from me, but don't mess me around.'

Before he can say anything, I storm down the pathway and hurry to catch up with Leroy and the others.

★ ★ ★

The waterfall and pool are two of the most beautiful things I've ever seen in my life. Leroy calls it 'The Hole', and it's easy to understand why. The cliff and waterfall open up into a stunning, turquoise-blue natural pool. There are vines hanging over the pool, and as I approach, Danny is already swinging from them and catapulting into the clear blue water below.

Lacey has shed her shorts and vest top and is wearing a cute pink bikini. I know she's been gifted it by a fashion company, and photos of her lounging in it will litter her feed as soon as we're back at the resort. Envy sprouts up inside me. I wish I still had that kind of confidence when it comes to posting.

Lacey waves at me before diving into the pool to meet Danny.

'Leroy!' she yells once she resurfaces. 'Will you take some photos, please?'

Leroy obliges and hurries around the edge of the pool to grab Lacey's camera. I watch as Danny swims over to her and, in one smooth movement, scoops her up in his arms. She shrieks, but her smile is wide as she wraps her arms around his neck and peppers his face with kisses.

I may not be Lacey's biggest fan right now, but they do make a cute couple.

Speaking of couples.

Cash appears next to me and nods his head appreciatively. 'It's beautiful.'

At least we can agree on that.

'You getting in?' he asks.

'No, I can't swim,' I remind him. 'I'll just swing my feet over the edge. But you go.' And then I add, because I'm worried that the others can hear us and might wonder why I sound like an HR professional while talking to my supposed boyfriend, 'Have fun.'

Cash hesitates, and for a moment, I think he's going to try and persuade me to jump in the pool with him or at least offer to sit with me, but he seems to decide against it. He shrugs and then sheds his shirt and shoes until he's only standing in a pair of shorts.

I pretend like I don't notice the way his shorts cling to him like a second skin and instead focus on glaring at a random spot on the ground.

As he scales the winding pathway to get to a higher point to jump into the pool, I make myself at home around the edge.

The water is the perfect temperature, and I let out a genuine sigh of relief as I dangle my legs into it. I grab my phone and take some videos of stunning surroundings and a few photos of me smiling up at the camera. Reluctantly, I even take one of Cash, capturing the moment he cannonballs into the pool and resurfaces, grinning from ear to ear like a child on Christmas morning.

He glances in my direction, and I quickly drop my phone into my lap and pretend to be fascinated with the lush greenery around us.

The plants around the pool shoot up high into the sky, creating a sort of cocoon effect that protects us from the sun and heat. I close my eyes and let my head loll backwards.

All my stress and anxiety about Cash, and Ethan, and The Video . . . it's all gone. I'm here, in the moment, and I'm enjoying it.

Until a wave of water suddenly sprays over me.

I snap my eyes open and find myself face-to-face with a grinning Cash.

'What the hell was that for?' I snap as he wades towards me.

'I've been trying to get your attention,' he says with a shrug. 'That was the only thing that worked.'

He swims up to me and gently pushes my legs apart to come and rest between my thighs. I try to push him away, but he brings his arms up to rest on my thighs and locks me in place. His fingers press into the soft skin there, and images from last night flash through my mind. I swallow.

'Bailey . . .' His voice is a low whisper like he's afraid the others will hear. 'I just wanted to say—'

'You've already said it,' I say quickly. I shift and clamp my thighs together so his hands slip off them. 'You don't need to keep repeating yourself. I get it.'

'No, you don't.' His hands come up to grip my thighs again like he's desperate to keep a hold of me somehow.

I huff in frustration and run a hand through my hair. 'I don't understand why you're fighting this.'

'Fighting what?'

I gesture between us. How can he not see it? How can he not *feel* it? 'This tension between us.' I lean forward, my breasts bumping gently against his chest, and stop when there are only a few millimetres between our noses. If I wanted to, I could easily drag my tongue down his jawline.

I think I do want to.

And I think he wants me to do it too. He shudders beneath me but doesn't move to push me away.

'I know you can feel it,' I murmur, my breath fanning across his face.

He still doesn't move. 'It doesn't matter what I feel.'

A familiar sting of rejection hits me, and *I* pull away. 'You want me.'

It's not a question. It's a fact, and he knows it. We both do. His body is betraying whatever crisis of respectability or morals he's currently going through.

'And I want you,' I continue. 'So let's do it. We're both consenting adults. Let's get it out of our systems, and then we can go back to the way things were.'

Cash's face twists into an expression I've not seen before. He looks almost pained.

'I don't *want* to get you out of my system, Bailey,' he says through gritted teeth.

'Then what do you want?'

'*That's the perfect shot!*'

Lacey's shriek of delight steals both of our attention. She's by the other end of the pool, but she's pointing at us with a huge smile on her face. 'The sun is hitting you two perfectly! You look like *the* hottest couple. Seriously, this could be a shot from a movie. Stay there. I'm going to get a shot for you guys. And then you get one of me and Danny after.'

'Lacey, it's fine,' I start to say, but she's already hopping out of the pool and grabbing her phone from Leroy.

'Come on,' Cash says quietly. He's not looking at me anymore. 'We still have to play the part, even if you're mad at me.'

'I'm not *mad* at you,' I hiss through a fake smile because Lacey is pointing her phone at us now. And I'm not. But I'm not sure what it is exactly that I am feeling. Disappointment maybe?

'Lean in a little closer,' Lacey continues to bark out orders. 'That's it. Lean in some more. Give us a kiss!'

I stiffen slightly as Cash tilts his head upwards. There's a spark in his eye, but he quickly blinks it away.

'Cash—' I begin.

'Don't worry,' he murmurs. He's stopped only an inch or two away from my lips, and his cool breath fans my cheeks as he speaks. 'I'm not going to kiss you. It just looks like I am. For the photo.'

I swallow and resist the sudden urge to close the gap between us and steal the kiss I've been craving. 'Got it.'

'Bailey,' he says, eyes serious. 'I need you to know something.'

The minuscule space between us is thick with tension. It feels like we're on the brink of something cataclysmic.

I lick my lips. His eyes follow my tongue as it darts out, and he inhales deeply.

'And what's that?' I ask.

His lip twitches, and I swear he's about to lean in and close the gap between us. But then, a strangled groan erupts from his mouth as Lacey's next shriek makes us jump apart.

'*Woohoo!* Our turn now! Bailey, come here and get some pics of me and Danny. I want the lighting to look *just* like yours. I'll send you your photos later. Cash, give me your Instagram, and I'll send them to you too.'

The distraction she's provided is a welcome one, and I leap away from Cash like I've been electrocuted.

I'm not sure I want to hear whatever it is he has to say. Because I know what it's going to be. He's even said it himself already today. I'm Dane's sister, and that's just not a line he's willing to cross.

Chapter Ten

Things are *different* between Cash and me now – which is fair, I suppose. The dynamics of our relationship with one another have been flipped over the last few days, and I'm not sure either of us knows how to proceed.

He keeps up the loving boyfriend act when we're in front of the others, but as soon as we're alone, it's like he can't get away from me quick enough. In a weird way, we're kind of right back to where we started. Which wouldn't be a problem if my feelings for *him* could go back to right where they started.

I'm sunbathing on the terrace of our suite after our hike and our day at the waterfall. Cash is nowhere to be seen. He came back to the suite with me but only stayed long enough to change his clothes. That was about an hour ago, and he's still not returned.

My phone vibrates on the small table next to me, and I jump. I hadn't realised it had reconnected to the WiFi.

One Week in Paradise

INSTAGRAM
597 notifications

I sit upright, my brows shooting up. Anxiety hits me like a wave as I tap on the app. It's been months since I've had a response like this on Instagram, and almost every single notification is for the post I'd shared earlier.

Most of the comments are positive.

@helena_yung21 *where is that dress from!! it's gorgeous!!*
@ashley.doe___ *omg Jamaica??? so jealous*
@queengracieeee *so happy to see you back on my feed again*
@curlsgirlscurls *hair looks stunning girl! drop the routine*

My heart swells as I scroll through them. For a moment, I wonder why I ever was so nervous about posting again. My audience is lovely and supportive and—

@gail23456862 *lol, she's at a couples resort but where's her man????*

@burner_420 *has she stolen another one?*

I quickly delete their comments and block both accounts, hoping that not too many people have seen them. *They're just trolls*, I remind myself as I scan through the rest of the comments to see if anything else jumps out at me. *Just stupid, sad little trolls.*

I try to focus on all the positive feedback I'm receiving. My DMs are filled with young women asking me about what products I'm using in my hair or where I got my dress from. There's even a brand or two in there asking for my details to send me products to try.

As I respond to the comments and questions filling up my DMs, my anxiety begins to fade away. Not all of it, but I immediately begin to feel lighter.

I'm back in my element.

This is what I do, and I'm good at it.

Influencers can get a bad rep sometimes, but I truly love what I do. Sometimes it feels like I've got a little community of sisters and cousins in my pocket, and I love sharing the things that bring me joy and make my life that little bit easier with them.

Once I've finished responding to everything, I put my phone down and lean back into my lounger. The sun is beating down on me, and in the distance, I can hear the waves crashing against the shore at the nearby beach.

I close my eyes and smile.

For the first time in months, I feel at peace.

★ ★ ★

That feeling of peace doesn't last long.

'Bailey? Are you sure you want to do this?'

I grit my teeth and then turn to face Cash. He's standing in front of me, looking stupidly attractive in a patterned silk button-down with a *very* low neckline. He holds his arms out and gives me a weak smile.

'It's not too late to turn back.'

But it is.

I sigh and take a step forwards, letting him loop one arm around my waist. His hand rests on my lower back, and I suddenly regret my decision to wear an open-back dress this evening. He holds out his other arm and wiggles his fingers at me.

Up until ten minutes ago, I'd forgotten that I'd signed us up for a couples dance class this evening. It's not until Penelope comes knocking on our suite door shortly after dinner to come and collect us that I remember what I've done.

'Come on,' Cash says, a wry smile tugging at his lips. 'I won't bite.'

But that's the problem, isn't it? I think I *want* him to.

And I think that's what's bothering me the most.

I don't want to be attracted to Cash. I don't want to look into his eyes and have my breathing stutter or my heartbeat quicken when I feel his hand rub up against my bare skin.

I want things to go back to normal. Back when Cash hated and ignored me, and I was immune to his ridiculous good looks.

But after everything that's happened between us so far on this trip, I don't think that's possible. Cash knows that I'm attracted to him, and he's lording it over me.

I scowl as he reaches for my hand and entwines our

fingers together. I hate that I've become just like every other girl in his life, throwing myself at him and feeding into his ego.

'Excellent form, you two!' our dance instructor, Claudia, tells us as she hurries around the veranda to help some of the other couples there. I spot Meera and Sara giggling together in a corner, and I throw them a wave.

Cash grins. 'I'm not used to you being this tall.'

That gets a snort out of me. I'm wearing a pair of heels, but I'm still several inches shorter than him. If I really wanted to, I could probably tuck my head under his chin.

'Now, *feel the rhythm*,' Claudia yells. She shuffles to the front of the veranda and begins stepping from side to side to the beat of the slow reggae song blasting from the speakers. 'Like this. Left. Right. Left. Right. Move your hips. Move together as one.'

Cash pulls me in so I'm flush against his chest, and he begins to mimic Claudia's movements. I'm happy to let him lead. I'm an awful dancer. And anyway, I'm secretly enjoying the feel of his muscles tensing and flexing underneath me as he shimmies from side to side.

Unlike me, he's a surprisingly good dancer. His hips move with a fluidity I never would have expected from him, and my thoughts immediately turn sensual.

A few strands of his hair fall loose from the messy bun he's pulled it into this evening. I lean into the urge I've been having since that meeting at the café. I reach up and ghost my fingers through his hair.

He inhales sharply but doesn't jerk away.

'It's so soft,' I marvel as I twist a strand around my finger. 'And so healthy. I'm impressed.'

Cash grins at me. 'Well, it should be. I'm just doing what you told me to.'

'Me?' I frown, trying to scour my memories for any hair recommendations I've ever given him. I come up blank.

'Not directly,' he admits. 'You posted something on Instagram a while back about this product you said would be good for people with my hair type.' He shrugs casually. 'I gave it a go, and it worked.'

A feeling of warmth cascades through my body, and for a moment, I'm speechless.

'You followed one of my recommendations?' I manage to choke out.

'Of course,' Cash says with another shrug like *I'm* the weird one for being surprised. 'You know what you're talking about, obviously. Why wouldn't I give it a try?'

Because, aside from Amber, nobody else in my life listens to me like that. Dad thinks my choice of career is a joke. Mum follows me on Instagram, but only out of sympathy and she's never bought any of the products I've recommended.

And Dane? Dane doesn't really ask any questions outside

of messaging me to ask if I have any discount codes on brands he likes.

'Thank you,' I mumble. I'm struck by just how much I mean it. 'You know, I didn't even realise that you follow me until a few days ago.'

'I've been following you for a while.'

'You should've said something.'

'Maybe I just like cheering you on from a distance.'

I shake my head and snort. 'I don't understand you, Cash.'

Claudia shouts out some more instructions, and he dips me slightly, his eyes on the long stretch of skin on my neck as he moves.

'What's not to understand?'

'One minute you hate me, the next—'

His eyes turn serious. 'Stop saying that. Why do you think I hate you?'

'Because you do,' I insist. 'I'm not stupid. I can tell.'

He laughs, but there's no humour in it. 'I don't hate you, Bailey. I can promise you that.'

'I don't hate you either.'

'That's good to know.'

The song blasting through the speakers changes suddenly to something more up-tempo, and Cash spins me around.

'I didn't peg you as a dancer,' I say. 'Is this what you and Dane get up to in the club?'

'Dane has two left feet,' Cash chuckles. 'He's a hazard on the dance floor. It must run in the family.' He gives me a pointed look, and I deliberately glance away.

'My mum taught me how to dance,' he continues. 'She feels very strongly that every man should be able to hold his own on the dance floor.'

The rhythm speeds up as the song hits the bridge, and Cash easily matches our stride with the tempo.

'That's how she and my dad met back in the day,' he explains. 'At a friend's wedding. They bumped into each other on the dance floor, and that was that.'

'That's really sweet.'

'Yeah.' Cash gives me a soft smile. 'They had a great relationship; from what I remember of it, anyway.'

'How old—'

'He died when I was nine,' Cash says, knowing what my question was going to be. 'So it's just been me and Mum ever since.'

'She did a great job with you,' I say softly, and I mean it too. I'm rapidly beginning to realise that the Cash I made up in my head – the egotistical asshole with no personality – is not the same person holding me right now.

There are layers to him, and I want to peel them all back and see what's at his core.

'I'm sorry about earlier,' I say, deciding it's time for me to do my part to mend this rift between us. 'I overstepped.

I get it, and you're right. You're Dane's best friend. I wouldn't want to ruin that over a stupid holiday fling.'

Cash swallows. 'Yeah. Exactly.'

'And promise me you won't tell Dane about any of this?' I grimace. 'He'll never let me live it down.'

We meet each other's gaze, and I have to focus, so I don't drown in his eyes.

'I promise,' he says. 'It'll be our secret.'

* * *

The dance class is more fun than I expect. We spend the night wrapped in each other's arms, swaying and moving to the rhythm of the songs on Claudia's playlist. Claudia dutifully takes loads of photos and videos of us, and I'm strangely excited to scroll through my camera roll and see them all later tonight.

When the session ends, we're not ready to head back to the suite, so we spend several hours aimlessly doing laps around the resort, talking about anything and everything.

I've known Cash for nearly two decades, but we've never spoken as much as we have tonight. I feel like I've been introduced to a completely new person.

He's open and honest with me, laughing freely as he tells me about his first-ever construction job and how he accidentally shot a nail through his thumb within the first hour.

'You can still kind of see the scar,' he says, wiggling his

thumb in front of my face. 'All right, it's your turn. That was my most embarrassing work story. What's yours?'

'That wasn't *embarrassing*,' I say. 'More like painful.'

'Fair,' he concedes. 'What about the time I was redoing a bathroom for a client, and I stepped out to get some fresh air, and when I came back, they were sitting on the toilet?'

'That's not too bad.'

'*Naked.*'

Laughter wracks through me. 'What the hell?'

'I know!' Cash laughs easily with me. 'They weren't even apologetic. They acted like *I* was the problem. Very weird. I left and didn't go back.'

'Understandable.'

'Your turn.'

I can't tell him my most embarrassing work story because that technically involves Ethan and the aftermath in the wake of The Video, and I'm not ready to relive that particular torture just yet. Instead, I tell him about the collaboration I did with a brand whose make-up gave me an allergic reaction.

'My lips were *so* swollen,' I groan as I take out my phone and show Cash one of the few photos I took. 'And it gave me this really horrible rash all over my face. I couldn't leave my place for a full week. And to make it worse, the make-up was genuinely terrible. It was so cakey and dry. They didn't believe me at first, so I had to send them the photos. It was so embarrassing.'

Cash doesn't laugh. In fact, he looks quite concerned. 'Did they compensate you?'

'Of course not,' I snort. 'They actually still wanted me to post a video. They thought the lips were giving Kylie Jenner and that it would be good for business.'

'Did you post?'

'Absolutely not. I couldn't recommend the brand to my audience in good faith. I gave them back their fee and told them they need to work on their formula some more.'

'What'd they say about that?'

'No response.'

Cash shakes his head in dismay. 'I'm glad you didn't post.'

'Of course; I've got integrity,' I say with a shrug. My lips turn upwards into a smirk, and I quirk a pointed brow. 'And besides, I can't lead my loyal fans, like you, astray.'

He mirrors my smirk. 'As head of your fan base, I'm glad to hear that.'

We fall into an easy banter, and I feel a pang of regret as it hits me that we could've had this all along. We could've been friends *years* ago.

'Be honest with me,' I say, deciding to bite the bullet.

'Always.'

'Why is this the first time we've done this?'

'Faked a relationship to get a free flight to Jamaica?'

I give him a look and gesture between us. 'No. You know what I mean. You and Dane have been best friends for years, and we barely know each other. To be honest, up until now, I was sure you hated me.'

'I've never hated you,' he repeats quietly.

'I know, I know, you've said. But it *feels* like you did. Like you could barely stand to be in a room alone with me before. I don't think we've ever exchanged more than twenty words between us until now. You can't blame me for thinking otherwise.'

Cash sighs and looks up at the clear night sky, his brows meeting in the middle as they furrow into a deep frown. 'Yeah, I see what you mean.'

'I prefer it like this,' I tell him earnestly. 'I think we make good friends.'

'Yeah,' he says, that frown still clouding his features. 'Great friends.'

★ ★ ★

I know how to walk in heels. I've been doing it since I was fifteen years old, and I'm pretty proud of my walk. I'm not like Naomi Campbell or anything like that, but I know how to hold my own in a pair of six-inch heels.

However, my feet are currently killing me. An evening of dancing and aimlessly strolling around the resort, chatting about our lives and goals, will do that to your toes.

There aren't any golf carts in the vicinity, so Cash and I are making our way back to the suite on foot.

'I'm taking these off,' I declare dramatically after two minutes of hobbling after him. The pain is too much to handle, and I'm throwing in the towel. I crouch down and start fiddling with the thin strap wrapped around my ankle. 'Hold up, let me unstrap these.'

'Your feet will get dirty.'

'Anything's better than this.' I manage to unstrap and hook one heel, but before I can get to the other one, a shadow looms over me.

'Let me carry you,' Cash says. He turns around and offers me his back. 'Hop on. Come on,' he adds, sensing my hesitation.

'Are you sure?'

'Come on, Bailey. It's getting late.'

I stand up as he crouches down and swing my legs over his waist. His hands come up to grip my thighs, and soon he's lifting me into the air. I wrap my arms loosely around his neck so that I don't fall back. Cash adjusts under me slightly, shifting his arms, so they create a little seat for me to lean into.

I'm suddenly acutely aware of just how close we are to one another now. My face is buried in his neck, his wavy hair tickling my nose with each step he takes. I wonder if he can feel my racing heartbeat thudding against his back.

'I'm not too heavy, am I?' I ask, more out of a desire to say anything and end the loaded silence between us than to actually know.

'Don't be ridiculous,' he says. 'You're perfect.'

My heart skips a beat. Does he know what he does to me when he says things like that?

I scoff into his neck. 'Don't say things you don't mean.'

'I never do.'

I squeeze his neck a little tighter, and we walk the rest of the way home in silence.

Chapter Eleven

When I wake up, Cash is still there. He's all the way over on his side of the bed, but a feeling of relief washes over me as I watch the slow rise and fall of his chest.

I'm glad we're in a better place together. The tension between us is still there, but it's becoming easier to push aside. I'm enjoying getting to know Cash, and I'm excited to see what I'll learn today.

He stirs and yawns, turning onto his side so he's facing me. He looks at me, eyes warm, mouth splitting into an easy, lazy smile. For a moment, it feels like I'm his whole world. And then he blinks and seems to remember where he is. He shoots upright and runs a hand through his messy locks.

'What time is it?' Cash's morning voice is low and husky, and it sends a jolt of warmth running through me, pooling in the pit of my stomach.

'Just gone eight,' I murmur.

He rubs the sleep out of his eyes. 'What're we doing today?'

I scroll through my phone quickly to find the itinerary Penelope sent over. 'A couples massage.'

He nods and moves to stand up but then quickly flops back into bed. Except he doesn't stick to his side. He rolls closer to where I am, tentatively stopping in the middle of the bed. 'Gimme five more minutes.'

'The massage isn't until twelve,' I tell him. There's still a decent distance between us, but if I wanted to, I could reach out and press my hand flat against his bare chest. The thought makes my throat constrict, and I swallow thickly. 'You can go back to bed. I'm gonna go and meet the others for breakfast.' I swing my legs out of bed and pad quickly to the bathroom.

'Are you sure?'

I manage to squeak out a *yes*, and hope that he doesn't notice how high my voice is. Those annoying sensual thoughts are back, and I need to push them away before I ruin everything.

★ ★ ★

Penelope is looking at me like she's about to tell me she was the one who ran over my childhood cat Hercules and left him to die in the street.

It's just before noon, and Cash and I are waiting outside the spa, ready to get our massages.

'Guys, I am *so* sorry,' she says, looking genuinely like she's about two seconds away from bursting into tears. 'The spa is closed today. Our masseuses had a family emergency, and they won't be in today. I can't tell you how sorry I am. And I know you were looking to film some content about the massage specifically.'

'It's fine,' I tell her. 'I hope the masseuses are okay?'

'Yes, they're fine. Just need to deal with some family arrangements. They'll be back tomorrow if you've got time then?' She groans and whacks her hand against her forehead. 'But no. You're booked for the tandem jet-skiing, aren't you?'

'Don't worry about it, Penelope,' I try to reassure her, this time a little more firmly. I can see that she's spiralling and worried I'll leave a bad review or put the resort on blast. 'We're having a great time. It's a shame about the massage, but it can't be helped. There's no need to worry.'

She still looks a little worried, but I think I've assuaged her fears for the most part. She spends another minute or two apologising and then hurries off to find Bea and Marcus, who are apparently going on a herb farm tour this afternoon.

'That's a shame,' I mumble once Penelope is out of earshot. 'I was really looking forward to that.'

The plan was to spend the afternoon getting the massages, then I was going to hang by the pool and read for the rest of the day. Since the other couples weren't going to be around, I told Cash he was free to disappear and do what he liked for the rest of the day, but he said he was happy to stick with me and have a pool day.

'You can still have a massage,' Cash says as we stroll back to our suite. 'You may don't know this about me, but I've been told I have magic hands.'

A nervous laugh escapes me. It's not that I haven't thought about his hands running over my body, but I'm desperately trying to keep those thoughts at bay, and Cash isn't helping. 'Who told you that?'

'Just people,' Cash says innocently. Girls, probably. Lots and lots of girls. 'Seriously, I give a pretty good massage.'

I glance at his hands and remember how they'd felt inching up my thighs that night at the cabana bar. 'I don't doubt it.'

I gasp and cover my mouth. I hadn't meant to say that out loud, but it's too late. Cash is grinning down at me, and I can see from the look in his eyes that this isn't a battle I'm going to win.

'Fine,' I say, trying my best to act like I'm doing *him* a favour. 'Let's see what you've got.'

Once we're back in the suite, Cash instructs me to take off my vest and lie face down on the bed. I do as he says and try to ignore the feeling of warmth that pools low in my belly when he tells me what to do. That's something for me to unpack later. *Much* later.

'You ready?' he asks.

I nod, not trusting my voice.

He crawls over me, knees on either side of my hips, and lowers himself down, so he's resting lightly on my ass.

'I'm not too heavy?' he asks.

'No,' I manage to croak out. 'You're perfect.'

That gets a chuckle out of him. 'I'll start with your back.'

He places his hands gently on my back, and I'm pleasantly surprised to feel that they're warm.

'Take a few deep breaths with me,' he says. 'In and out until we're in sync.'

I feel myself pulse down there as I blindly follow another one of his orders. Maybe I need to unpack this now. Why does him telling me to do something send a jolt of arousal shooting through me like this?

We take deep breaths together until we're breathing as one.

'Good girl,' he mumbles, and that truly nearly sends me over the edge. I bury my face in a pillow to muffle my groan and hope that he doesn't notice the way I'm squeezing my thighs together.

Once he's happy with our breathing, he brings his hands to rest at the base of my neck, his thumbs pressing gently on my spine. I inhale a sharp breath as he glides his hands all the way down my back, right down to the curve of my ass. For a second, I think he's about to squeeze my cheeks, but then his hands move out to my hips, and he presses his thumbs into the soft skin on my sides.

It feels sensational. Every ounce of stress and anxiety I've been clinging to for the last three months fades away with his touch, and I feel myself sinking into the mattress as my entire body turns to jelly.

His hands move up towards my shoulder blades, his palms making small circles along my back as he goes. 'Does this feel good?'

'*Yes.*' And I can't help the loud groan that escapes from my lips as his hands slide back down my back again, gliding over the curve of my ass. *Lower.* I need him to go lower. I lift my hips slightly, my back arching into his touch and moan, 'Yes, you feel so good.'

His hands freeze, and I hear his breath hitch. Then suddenly, the bed creaks and the weight of his body on top of mine is gone. I glance over my shoulder. Cash is standing away from the bed. His face is red, and he's breathing heavily.

'You okay?' I ask.

'Mhm,' he hums. I don't miss the way his voice cracks slightly.

'Are you sure? You don't look—'

'I'm fine,' he chokes out. He stumbles backwards until his back hits the bathroom door. 'The massage is over, by the way. I think I'm going to have a shower.'

I blink at him, my mind still a little bit hazy. '*Now?*'

'Yeah, it's pretty hot, and I'm sweaty, and I feel gross and . . .' He trails off as he opens the bathroom door and disappears inside.

I lay there on the bed and try not to think about how incredibly turned on I am right now.

I fail.

Miserably.

As soon as I hear that he's got the shower running, I flip onto my back and immediately hike my skirt up. I dip my hand past the waistband of my panties and heave a sigh of relief as I press against my throbbing pussy. I don't think I've ever been this wet before.

I close my eyes and try to pretend like it's Cash's hand down there.

Good girl.

I imagine he's on top of me, whispering orders to me and heaping me with praise when I comply. I take my free hand and stick two of my fingers in my mouth. I run my tongue along them until they're dripping and then bring the fingers down to my nipples, pretending like they're Cash's tongue lapping over my breasts.

I keep my thumb on my clit and slide two fingers inside myself, and imagine it's Cash inside me, filling me up as the walls of my pussy squeeze around him.

'Oh, *Cash*.' His name spills from my lips as I come, long and hard, around my fingers.

I don't know how long I lay there, panting and moaning as I ride out the blissful waves of my orgasm, but when I open my eyes, Cash is standing in front of me, mouth open, eyes hazy.

The imprint of his dick is clear against the towel he has wrapped around his waist.

He's hard.

'*Bailey*,' he croaks. 'Shit. I'm sorry. I should've told you I was coming back in.'

My cheeks flush. I still haven't moved. I'm lying here, one hand on my naked breasts, the other stuffed into my panties. I squeeze my legs shut and roll into the blankets to cover myself.

'I'm gonna—' He swallows. 'I'll let you—' And then Cash is gone, back into the bathroom.

I sink back into the blankets and groan. For some reason, I can't help but feel like I've been rejected.

Chapter Twelve

'He watched you doing *what?*'

'*Sssh!*' I hush Amber and peek out of the large window onto the terrace. Cash is doing laps in the infinity pool outside our suite. Once I'm sure he hasn't heard Amber's outburst, I turn my attention back to my phone. 'And he wasn't *watching* me. He just caught me.'

'That is . . .' Amber pauses for a second, pondering on what word to choose. 'Extremely hot. Damn.'

'Tell me about it.'

I know that I should probably feel embarrassed or ashamed that Cash has caught me in such a compromising and vulnerable position, but I don't. The arousal he felt watching me was evident, and I'd be a liar if I said it didn't turn me on even more.

'Have you spoken about it?' Amber asks.

'No. He basically ran away once I realised that he was

there.' I sigh and flop onto the comfortable couch. 'And now he's acting like it never happened.'

'You guys are ridiculous,' Amber snorts. 'Just fuck each other already.'

'We've already decided we're not doing that,' I tell her. 'His friendship with Dane is too important to ruin with a fling.'

'So you're just gonna spend the rest of your time in Jamaica running around like the unresolved sexual tension between you two isn't off the charts?'

'Yes. Exactly.'

'You guys are ridiculous.'

She's right. But I don't think I'd ever be able to forgive myself if I ruined Cash and Dane's friendship just because I'm horny.

'It's for the best,' I tell her. Amber looks like she wants to say more, but I cut her off with a quick change of topic. 'Did you see my last post?'

'Yes! It was great, and not too many troll comments either this time.'

The troll comments on my posts *are* easing up. There seem to be a few dedicated assholes committed to bringing up Ethan or The Video every time I post anything, but the positive comments definitely outweigh them all. Even my follower account is steadily increasing. I'm back up to 232,349. Still a far cry from my peak, but I'm definitely getting there again.

'People love seeing you happy,' says Amber. 'That's what I've been trying to tell you. You just made yourself look guilty by hiding and going offline. Act like it doesn't bother you, and people will forget things.'

I know she's making sense, but I can't help but feel guilty for my part in everything that happened. The troll comments are my punishment for that. But I haven't told Amber about it yet, and now isn't the time.

Cash pokes his head through the sliding doors and waves to get my attention. 'The others are all hanging out here. You want to come and join?'

I look over his shoulder. Marcus, Danny and Sara are diving into the pool while Bea, Lacey and Meera relax on sun loungers.

I end the call with Amber, promising to keep her updated on any developments between Cash and me (as unlikely as that may be, but it gets her off my back), and change into a bikini.

When I get outside, Cash, Marcus and Danny are in the middle of a 'hold your breath underwater' competition. As I approach the sun loungers, Lacey tilts her head down and peers at me over the top of her large, cat-eye sunglasses. I offer her a wave, but it's not returned.

I shrug off the odd energy emanating from Lacey and slide into an empty sun lounger between Meera and Bea.

'You not getting in?' I ask.

'No way,' says Bea. 'I'm more of a "lounge by the pool and look cute" kind of girl.'

'Agreed,' says Meera.

I laugh. They're both certainly succeeding.

We watch as the guys start a race in the pool, seeing who can do ten laps the fastest. Cash easily cuts through the water, and the sight of him, wet and glowing in the sunlight, nearly makes me malfunction.

I've got to get myself under control.

'What've you all been up to today?' I ask. 'We were supposed to have the couples massage, but it got cancelled.'

'Same,' says Sara. 'I was really looking forward to it.'

'We did the massages yesterday,' says Bea. 'It was *amazing*. Very romantic.' She peeks over the ridge of her knees to see where the guys are. Satisfied that they're not within earshot, she drops her voice to a conspiratorial whisper. 'Marcus hasn't been able to keep his hands off me. I don't know what they put in that oil, but it did the damn job.'

'Massages can be *very* sensual when done properly,' Meera says. 'It's such a shame they had to cancel. What have you and Cash been up to instead, Bailey?'

My mind flashes back to earlier this afternoon. Cash crouching over me, his hands deftly making their way down my back.

I clear my throat and hope I can blame the sun for my

rapidly reddening cheeks. 'Not much. Just relaxing in our suite.'

Sara wiggles her brows. 'Is that a euphemism *or* . . .'

'What do you mean?'

'You know,' Sara says with a sly shrug. 'You and Cash . . . getting to know each other.'

'Yeah,' says Meera. 'How are things going? Are the sparks flying?'

Bea lets out a cackle. 'I think things are going pretty well for the new couple.'

My cheeks are on fire. 'What's that supposed to mean?'

Bea lolls her head in my direction and gives me a knowing look. 'Come on, girl. We all saw you last night at the dance lesson.'

'You couldn't keep your hands off each other,' says Meera.

'It was a dance lesson,' I protest. 'Where were our hands supposed to be?'

Bea hums, and the three of them share a glance. 'I'm just saying. He can't keep his eyes off you.'

'We're not trying to embarrass you,' says Meera. She reaches over and gives me a gentle nudge. 'I just . . . We know it's not been easy for you recently after everything that happened. We just want to make sure you know you've got a good thing in front of you. Sometimes it can be hard to see.'

A lump forms in my throat. It seems like Cash and I have

been playing the perfect couple, much better than I'd expected.

'They're right.'

I jump at the sound of Lacey's voice. She's been so quiet the entire time I've forgotten that she's here.

'Cash *is* quite the catch,' she says slowly, her tone careful and considered. 'Where did you say you guys met again?'

Before I can answer, Cash swims up to the edge of the pool and grins at me. I can't help but smile back.

'Oh, good. Cash is here too.' She leans forward and rests her chin on her interlaced fingers. Then she smiles at him, but it's not her normal wide smile. It's cold and calculating, and it sends a shiver down my spine.

If Cash notices that Lacey's tone is a little off, he doesn't let it show. He hoists himself out of the pool and plops down onto the sun lounger, lifting my legs up and dropping them onto his lap.

'Remind us all again,' Lacey says. 'How did you two meet?'

I meet Cash's gaze for a half second, panic flitting across my features. It's a huge oversight, but we never actually sat down and decided what our 'getting together' story would be.

'We met on—' I begin, but Cash cuts across me.

'Her brother is my best friend.'

My brows shoot up. Okay. So we're going with a version of the truth.

Cash glances over at me, and a slow smile spreads across his face. 'I guess I've always had a thing for her, but I wasn't sure if she ever actually liked me.'

I swallow. Cash is looking at me like he means it. Like he *really* means it.

'So I've always just kind of admired her from afar,' he finishes with a small shrug.

'Aw, you *guys*,' Meera trills. 'That is so cute! What made you finally give him a chance, Bailey?'

Everyone turns to face me, and it feels like there's a spotlight shining directly on me. I ignore them all as best I can and focus entirely on Cash. I know that he's just playing the part of a doting boyfriend in front of the others and that he doesn't *really* mean what he's just said, but I can't stop my truth from spilling from my lips.

'Once I got to know him – the *real* him – I couldn't help falling for him.'

'Isn't that just *adorable*?' Lacey says, her voice void of any emotion. She narrows her eyes as she looks between Cash and me. 'What a perfect couple.'

I throw her a weird look. I don't know what's gotten into her today, but I don't like it. She seems bothered by our presence for some reason.

Cash gives my leg a gentle squeeze and then dives back into the pool.

Danny has found a beach ball, and they've started up

a game of volleyball. Meera and Sara both dive in, and with some coaxing from Marcus, Bea tentatively joins them too.

'Are you not going to get in?' Lacey asks me after a beat or two of awkward silence.

It's just the two of us now lying across our loungers.

I shake my head. 'I can't swim. Look, Lacey, is everything all right?'

She tilts her head to the side, her lips twisting into a small smirk. 'How do you mean?'

'Something seems off between us. If you've got something to say, just say it.'

I don't expect her to do it, but to her credit, she does. 'I saw The Video. The one that went viral.'

My stomach drops. 'Okay. And?'

'*And?*' she scoffs before flopping back down onto her sun lounger. 'I don't associate with cheaters. Girls like you are the *worst*.'

'*I* wasn't the cheater,' I say through gritted teeth. I can't believe this is still coming up. 'Ethan was. And I was just as much a victim as the other girl was.'

Lacey doesn't say anything, and anger surges through me. Will I ever be free from this label?

'I don't care if you don't believe me,' I say. 'It's the truth.'

Lacey glances my way, arching a perfect blonde brow.

'You know, after I watched The Video, I realised something. I know the girl in it. Not you, the other one. Ethan's *actual* girlfriend.'

My blood runs cold.

'She's a friend of one of my cousins. I reached out to her and asked her what happened, and she told me *everything*.'

Everything.

She says that word so slowly, letting each excruciating syllable hang in the air.

'I know what you did, Bailey. You're not as innocent as you like to pretend. Does he know?' She nods over to where Cash is tossing the ball to Sara.

'Please don't say anything,' I whisper. Out of everything that's happened since The Video went viral, I think Cash knowing the truth might just be the worst thing. Any goodwill I've acquired during this trip will evaporate in an instant. He'll tell Dane. Dane will tell Mum. Mum will tell Dad. And I'll never be able to escape their disappointed stares and mumbles for the rest of my life.

'God, you're pathetic.'

Pathetic.

She's right. She turns away from me and pulls her sunglasses over her eyes. I've been dismissed.

Despite the heat, my entire body feels cold. I push myself up from the lounger, blinking back tears as I walk rigidly back to our suite.

'What's up, Bailey?' Cash calls from the other end of the pool.

'Got a bit of a headache,' I mumble. 'I think the heat's getting to me. I'm gonna lie down for a bit.'

I don't wait for his response. As soon as I'm back inside our suite, I pull the curtain over our large sliding doors and submerge the whole room in darkness.

Once I'm sure I'm hidden from the others, I crawl into bed, hug my knees to my chest, and let the tears fall.

Chapter Thirteen

I spend the rest of the day in bed.

Cash is kind enough to give me all of twenty minutes to myself before he slips quietly into the suite. I've wrapped myself in a cocoon of blankets, and I don't turn to look at him as he enters.

'Bailey?' he says, his voice quiet and uncertain. 'Are you all right? Do you need me to get you anything? Paracetamol? Water?'

'I'm fine,' I rasp, wincing as I hear myself. It's obvious that I've been crying. I cough to try and mask the obvious emotion in my voice. 'Go back outside with the others.'

There's a moment of silence, and then his footsteps pad closer towards the bed. The mattress dips slightly, and I realise that he's crawled onto it.

'Cash—'

I freeze, my voice locking in my throat. Cash has slipped under the blankets and pulled me flush against his chest. His arms wrap around me, and he gives me a gentle squeeze. 'You're okay, Bailey. You're okay.'

The floodgates immediately open, and I bawl into his chest. He doesn't say a word. He just lays there, gently rubbing my back as I incoherently wail. I don't think anyone's ever been this gentle or patient with me before.

When my sobs eventually die down and become infrequent sniffles, Cash pulls back slightly and rubs a thumb along my tear-stained cheeks.

'You want to talk about it?'

I shake my head. 'Not yet.'

I expect him to push, but all he says is, 'Okay,' and we fall back into an easy silence.

'Are you sure you don't want to go back outside?' I ask, my voice slightly muffled in his chest. 'Seriously, you don't have to wait in here with me.'

'I want to,' he says simply.

I curl myself closer to his chest. The sound of his heartbeat against my ear is oddly soothing. 'I'm sorry,' I murmur.

'Nothing to be sorry about.'

'You're wasting your holiday in here with me. You should be out there, enjoying the sun.'

'I already told you,' he says. 'I want to be here. Stop trying to push me away. Let me be here for you.'

My heart swells with . . . What is that? Warmth? Gratitude? Love? 'Okay.'

It feels like I belong here, nuzzled against Cash's chest. His body is warm beneath mine, and I never want to let go. 'I could fall asleep like this,' I murmur against his chest.

'Go on then,' he says softly. 'I'll be here when you wake up.'

'You promise?'

He leans forward and presses his lips against my forehead. The touch is so fleeting. For a second, I'm sure I've imagined it, but it sends shockwaves running through my body.

'I'm not going anywhere, Bailey.'

★ ★ ★

He keeps his promise.

When I wake hours later, Cash is still curled up beside me. One hand is wrapped around me, and the other is gently combing through my hair. He gives me a lazy smile as I shake off the sleep and blink up at him.

'Hey.'

I return the smile. 'Hey.'

'You feeling any better?'

'A little,' I say. Lacey's words are still there, looming in the back of my mind, but I feel safe here with Cash.

'Do you want to talk about it?'

I feel like I owe him the truth. Or at least some version of it. 'I'm guessing you know about my ex, Ethan?'

Cash nods. 'I've seen photos of you two together, and I know you had a messy break-up.'

'That's putting it lightly. He was cheating on me the entire time we were together.' I take a deep breath, steeling myself for the next part. 'And *I* was the other woman.'

I bury my face in Cash's chest to stop myself from looking up at him. I don't want to see the disgust or judgement that must be flitting across his face right now.

'I swear, I didn't know,' I say hurriedly. 'He's a photographer and gets a lot of work from high-fashion brands, so he was always travelling to Paris for work. I never suspected that he was really going back and forth to see his long-term girlfriend who lives there.'

Now that I've started talking, the words flow freely, and I feel a sense of relief as they come out. 'She eventually caught on somehow and realised something wasn't right. She flew to London to confront him and caught us having dinner. She came storming up to our table and went on this wild rant accusing me of being a home-wrecker.' I pause, my heart thudding as I recall every painful second of that night. 'Then she threw a glass of wine all over me. She was recording on her phone the whole time, and when she uploaded it online, it went viral.'

'Is that why you've been so quiet online recently?' Cash asks.

I nod. 'I don't come off very well in The Video. I'm

shouting back at her, telling her to get lost. And Ethan doesn't even try and defend me. He immediately chases after her when she eventually leaves. It makes me look really guilty and everyone immediately believed her side of the story. It went viral, and overnight, nobody wanted anything to do with me.'

I tell him about how my face was plastered over gossip blogs for weeks and how my comments were filled with nasty trolls calling me all kinds of cruel and untrue names.

I lean back and force myself to look into his eyes. 'But I didn't – I would *never*—'

'I know,' he says.

He says it like it's the most simple thing in the world. Like there's no doubt in his mind that he knows I would never purposely ruin a relationship. Other than Amber, he's the only person who knows who has immediately reacted like this. There's no sign of judgement or disgust in his gaze. Just pure, raw acceptance and kindness.

It makes my stomach flip.

I look away before I do something stupid, like lean in and kiss him.

'Most people aren't as nice as you,' I say quietly. 'Especially Lacey. Turns out she's an acquaintance of Ethan's *real* girlfriend, and she thinks I'm just the worst person in the world.'

'She should take a look in the mirror.'

I don't say anything because guilt has begun to gnaw at

me. There's something else I need to tell him, but I can't bring myself to do it. Because when I do, everything will change. He'll be on Lacey's side just like everyone else, and I'm not ready to let go of this tentative friendship we've built just yet. I want to hold onto it for as long as I can.

'Are you hungry?' he asks suddenly, sensing my apprehension to talk any further about Ethan. 'Let's order room service.'

He grabs the phone on his bedside table, and thirty minutes later, we're sitting up in bed with a tray of food and snacks in front of us.

I can't get over the sense of comfort that blankets me as we dig into our meal, like this is something we've done thousands of times before. I can immediately picture us sitting squashed together in bed back home in London, with a pizza box between us and the latest Netflix sensation running on the TV in front of us.

I realise, with a jolt, that I want that.

We're splitting our dessert – a ridiculously delicious vanilla layered berry cake – when Cash's phone vibrates.

He glances at it and immediately picks it up. 'It's my mum. Do you mind if I—'

'No, not at all. Go for it.' I shift a little to the side so I'm not in frame when Cash answers the call.

'Hello, my heart,' Cash's mum's voice crackles out through the speakers. 'How are things? Are you wearing sun cream every day and hydrating properly?'

'Hey, Mum,' Cash says, the tips of his ears turning pink. 'Everything's fine. Yes, every day. Yes, plenty of water.' He gives me a subtle eye roll, and I have to stuff a piece of cake into my mouth to smother my laugh. 'How're you?'

I can't help but glance over at the screen. Cash's mum is an adorable-looking woman with a head of long salt-and-pepper-flecked hair and kind green eyes. I can see so much of her in Cash's face.

'. . . Bailey?'

The use of my name snaps me back to attention.

Cash clears his throat. 'She's here with me right now. We're having a room service night.' He tilts his phone towards me, and I have half a second to school my expression into something that doesn't scream pure terror.

'Hello, sweet Bailey,' Cash's mum says. Her ruby lips are stretched into a wide smile. 'Still so beautiful. All that sun is doing you well, darling.'

'Hi, Mrs Reid,' I say with a nervous laugh. I don't think I've ever directly spoken to her before, but I remember her face from all the times she picked Cash up from our home growing up or dropped Dane off after a day at theirs. 'It's so lovely to see you.'

'Are you having a good time?' she asks. 'I hope my son has been treating you well on your trip.'

'He's been the perfect gentleman,' I say truthfully. 'We had a dance class last night.'

'A *dance class*?' Her eyes light up. 'You know, dancing is the best way to learn everything you need to know about a man? Does he know how to lead but also know how to let you shine? All very important things to know about a man, my dear.'

My lips twitch, threatening to pull into a smile. 'I'll keep that in mind.'

'I'm really enjoying all the photos Caspian has been sending me,' she says. 'You both look like you're having a wonderful time.'

Photos?

'We are,' I say. 'The resort is stunning, and the company isn't too bad either.'

'I'll let you two get back to your evening now. Give my love to Dane when you get the chance, and tell your parents I said hello. And *Caspian*,' she says suddenly. He turns the phone back to himself. 'Remember what I told you.'

'Yeah, yeah,' he mumbles. His face is so red. It looks like he's been out in the sun all day. 'I will. Talk to you later, Mum. Bye, love you.'

They say their farewells, and he ends the call. 'Sorry about that.'

'It's fine,' I say. I scoot a little closer to him in the bed until our arms brush against each other. 'What did she tell you?'

'Nothing,' he says quickly. Too quickly. 'Just more reminders about wearing sun cream.'

Hm. He's lying, clearly. But I decide, given how nice he's been to me this evening, to let it go. Instead I ask the next pressing question I have. 'What photos have you been sending her?'

He hesitates and then opens up his camera roll. It's filled with lots of beautiful landscape shots of our surroundings or overhead shots of the delicious meals we've been eating. It's also filled with photos of *me*.

Me, laughing at something.

Me, posing with Bea and Sara.

Me, sipping a cocktail.

Me, taking a photo of myself.

Me, red-faced and out of breath on our hike.

Me, sitting by the edge of the pool, my legs submerged in the clear water.

And us.

There's the photo we took when we landed, just outside the airport, our cheeks pressed together as we smile up at the camera. But there are more. His camera roll is filled with photos of us I hadn't even realised had been taken.

'Penelope, Meera and Bea have been sending me any photos they've taken of us,' Cash explains quickly, apparently sensing my confusion.

There's us on our first night at the resort, sitting at the cabana bar with everyone. I'm draped over Cash's waist, his hand on my thigh. Heat scorches through me as I remember where that evening led. I quickly swipe to the next photo.

It's the one Lacey took of us on our hike of Cash leaning into me like we're about to kiss. The next bunch are all from our dance class, and I can't help but smile as I scroll through them. He's holding me close in every single one, and I'm looking up at him like the world will fall apart if I dare to look away.

I hadn't even realised the others were taking photos of us the entire time.

'You'll have to send me all of these,' I tell him as I finish scrolling through them all. 'There are some real gems in here. We look so happy in all of them.'

'I am happy,' he says with a shrug.

And, you know what? I am too.

Chapter Fourteen

Cash is wearing an oversized, cheesy Hawaiian-style shirt, criminally short dark blue shorts, and a pair of oversized cheap, pink sunglasses. I should not be attracted to him right now, but I am.

Irrevocably so.

Today is jet-ski day. I eye the sea warily as our little group traipses down the beach to the landing area. I know my fears are irrational and unfounded, but I can't help the trepidation I feel as I watch the waves crash into the shore.

'You'll have a life jacket,' Cash says, effortlessly reading my thoughts.

'I know. I'm still nervous, though.'

'I'll be there with you,' he says with a shrug. 'Remember, I'm on shark watch this week. You'll be safe with me.'

'Thanks.'

We head down to the furthest end of the beach where

there's a jetty with several jet-skis lined up. Penelope waves us over.

'Afternoon, everyone! We've got an exciting few hours planned for you all. This is David.' She gestures to the tall man standing beside her. 'He's going to get you all sorted and strapped into your life jackets. Who wants to go first?'

Marcus storms forward, eager to get started.

Bea rolls her eyes. 'He's been looking forward to this since we got the invite.'

She joins him at the jetty, and David quickly gets them both into life jackets and settles them on one of the jet-skis. Lacey and Danny are up next, followed by Meera and Sara.

By the time our turn comes around, I'm almost shaking with nerves.

'We don't have to do this,' Cash says. 'We can just chill on the beach all day.'

'No, I want to.' And I do. It looks like fun, and I know my fears are irrational. These waters aren't filled with sharks (I know because I asked Penelope), and my life jacket will save me if I do happen to fall in. Still . . . 'Just – Just don't let me fall in the water, okay?'

Cash grins. 'I won't.'

He takes my hand and doesn't let go as we climb onto the rickety jetty. David suits us up quickly and directs us to the last jet-ski. Cash hops onto the front, and David helps lower me onto the back end. As soon as my butt touches the wet seat, I wrap my arms around Cash's waist and hold on tightly. He reaches an arm behind and gives my thigh a squeeze.

Lacey and Danny are on the jet-ski next to us, and I can feel her burning gaze on me. I don't look at her. I only have energy for one thing right now, and that's holding onto Cash as he begins to slowly inch us forward.

We all keep our speed quite low until we're far enough from the shoreline to avoid accidentally bumping into any swimmers. As soon as we hit that sweet spot, Marcus zooms forward, sending a spray of foamy water into the rest of us.

'You ready?' Cash asks.

I squeeze my eyes shut. 'Just go.'

Cash grips the handles tightly, and then we're off, gliding through the choppy waters. My shriek gets stuck in my throat as we hit a particularly bumpy patch and soar into the air I grip Cash even tighter, but he doesn't seem to mind.

Cash is in his element. His cheers are so loud, I can hear them over the sound of the engine and the roar of the waves. I feel a pang of desire as he glances back at me, a wide grin on his face.

'How're you enjoying it?'

To be honest, I'm terrified. Even without my irrational fear of sharks to keep me on edge, hurtling through the water at ridiculously high speed is not an activity that's high on my to-do list. But with Cash, I feel safe. I know, without a shadow of a doubt, that he won't do anything to put me in harm's way out here.

'It's not as bad as I thought it would be,' I tell him. Tentatively, I throw an arm into the air and mimic Cash's delighted cheer.

We swap positions halfway through, and Cash lets me take the lead.

He's incredibly patient as I slowly navigate the jet-ski and work up the courage to go faster than a snail. He doesn't mind how jerky and nervous I am, and his compliments flow freely whenever I do something right.

We zoom around for another half hour or so, and by the time we make land again, you never would've guessed that I'd been so apprehensive about the whole thing in the first place.

We split up with the others once we're done with the jet-skiing. Meera and Sara and Bea and Marcus head down to the other end of the beach for scuba diving lessons. Lacey doesn't say a word to me as she flounces past us and heads back to the resort with Danny hot on her heels.

Once it's just the two of us, Penelope directs us to a more secluded area of the beach away from the bustling crowds. She leads us around a corner and shows us a patch of glorious white sand with an umbrella of lush-looking plants and flowers hanging over it to keep the space separate from the rest of the beach.

Cash and I set up camp underneath a particularly leafy palm tree. The sand here is cool, a welcome change from the unrelenting heat blasting down on us.

Cash has shed his cheesy Hawaiian shirt, and it takes more effort than I'd like to admit to keeping my eyes off him. He's tanning nicely, his olive skin now a shade darker than usual. He stretches out in front of me, his long legs digging into the golden sand, and my gaze dips below his navel.

Those shorts he's wearing should be illegal.

It's not fair.

They show off his large, strong thighs and leave way too much room for my incredibly horny imagination to run wild.

'I'm going to get in the water,' Cash says, pulling me out of what are rapidly becoming extremely dirty thoughts. He's standing up now, wiping the sand off his body. 'Try and cool down a bit. Do you want to come? I *know* you can't swim,' he adds quickly, already knowing what my next words are going to be. 'But we won't go in too deep.'

I remember how safe he made me feel on the jet-ski and decide to continue to put my trust in him. 'Okay. But as soon as it hits my knees, I'm turning back.'

Cash grins and offers me a hand to pull me up. He keeps a hold of my hand as we approach the shoreline. As anxious as I currently feel about wading into such a large body of water, I'm suddenly filled with a sense of awe and wonder.

I don't think I've ever seen anything so beautiful before.

The crystal-clear water laps against the white sand, and the gentle sound of the waves drowns out the laughter and music coming from the beach around the corner. It's like we're in our own personal little bubble. And there's nowhere I'd rather be right now.

I squeeze Cash's hand as we approach the water's edge. The cool water hits my toes and sends a shiver up my spine.

'Ready?'

I nod and let Cash guide me into the ocean. The water washes over me, and I feel weightless. Free. Like nothing else in the world matters outside of this moment.

We walk until the water hits my knees. 'That's as far as I go.'

'We can go further,' Cash says. He glances back at me and shoots me a devilish grin. 'What if I carry you?'

Before I can counter, he twists slightly so he's standing in front of me. 'Just hold on to me,' he murmurs.

That sense of complete and utter safety washes over me again, and I do as he says. I wrap my arms around his neck, pulling my body flush against his.

Something flickers in his eyes, and they darken ever so slightly. His hands ghost down the length of my body, stopping at my butt. Then he hoists me up, and my legs instinctively wrap around his waist.

The gentle waves crash against us as we stand there, staring at each other.

I can feel his heartbeat and time my breathing to each slow thud. The sound of the waves crashing around us dulls to a low murmur, and all I can hear is his heartbeat thudding against my chest.

He takes a step backwards, and I cling to him a little tighter.

'Don't choke me,' he croaks.

'Don't drop me,' I counter.

'I'd never,' he says, voice dripping with sincerity. 'You're safe with me, Bailey. I promise.'

I squeeze him again. Not because I'm afraid he'll drop me and I'll plunge to my watery doom, but because I can't get close enough. The water is cold, but my skin is scorching, and I know his feels the same.

We stare into each other's eyes. I don't think we've ever been *this* close before. We're so close I can count the tiny constellation of freckles that pattern his jawline.

I wonder what he sees as he's looking at me. His grey-green eyes are hazy, almost drunk, as if he's drinking me in and can't get enough.

The thought sends shockwaves of desire shooting through me.

'God, Bailey,' he mutters, his voice lower than I've ever heard it. 'You're beautiful.'

And then he's kissing me.

My heart swells, but I have no time to react as his lips find purchase against mine. Something about this – his lips sliding against mine — feels natural, feels *right*, like it's something we should've been doing for years.

There's no force behind this kiss. It's gentle. Almost hesitant. Like he's giving me the opportunity to pull away and act like this never happened.

I do no such thing.

I angle my head downwards slightly, pressing my lips firmly against his, giving him the go-ahead. I can *feel* his hum of approval in my throat as his hands tighten around my ass and squeeze, pulling me even closer still.

I never want this to end. I move my lips against his, greedily taking in as much as I can before we need to come up for air.

'I've wanted to do that for *so long*,' he murmurs, his voice still a low groan.

'Me too,' I admit.

I pull him in for another kiss. This one is different from the first. The apprehension he began with is gone, replaced with a fiery desire. His fingers dig into my cheeks as he pulls me closer until there's not a millimetre of space between us. I moan and rock into him, and he takes the opportunity to slide his tongue into my mouth. We develop an easy rhythm, our tongues sliding against the other as we claw at each other in the middle of the ocean.

He pulls away from me for half a second, and the *mewl* that comes out of my mouth is desperate and whiny. I don't want him to stop. I lean forward, peppering his neck with tiny kisses, and he groans low in his throat.

I feel like I'm drowning in him, and I'm perfectly okay with that.

'*Fuck*,' he groans.

'Yeah,' I pant.

'We should go. It's getting dark.'

I look up. The sky is a mix of blues and purples. When did it get so late? How long have we been out here? I glance at my fingertips – they've begun to prune.

He's right. We *should* go. But I don't want to.

'No,' I say, more voice coming out in a pained whine. 'I don't want this to end.'

I'm content to stay in this moment with Cash for the rest of my life.

The look he gives me sends a shockwave of arousal through me. It's dark and sultry and filled with want and desire. 'I didn't say anything about stopping this.'

A shiver wracks through my body as he brushes his lips against my ear and whispers, 'As soon as we get back to the suite, I'm making you mine.' He pulls back and quirks a brow. 'You still want to stay out here?'

I shake my head.

His lips curl into a smile. 'Good girl.'

He walks us back to the beach. Once we hit the shallows, he doesn't put me down. Instead, he swivels me around in his arms, carrying me bridal-style out of the water. We quickly redress, barely caring that we're still soaked from the ocean, grab our belongings and head back towards the resort in silence, scared to say anything that will break the tension that lingers between us.

By the time we make it back to the room, I'm surprised my heart hasn't burst through my ribcage. The level of desire I'm feeling for him is unnerving. I've never felt like this with anyone before.

As soon as the door closes behind us, Cash's lips are on mine again. He easily hoists me up without breaking contact and walks us over towards the couch. I try and slide the sleeves of the cheesy Hawaiian shirt off his shoulders, but he jerks my hands away.

'Mm mm.' He shakes his head and hums against my lips. 'You first.'

He drops me onto the couch and hovers between my legs. My heart beats erratically as I look up at him.

He reaches up and cradles my jaw. His face is flushed, his lips are swollen, and he's looking at me like he can't wait to devour me. 'Do you remember that first night at the bar?'

I nod. How could I forget?

'Let's finish what we started.' He rubs his thumb over my lips, and I dart my tongue out to lick it.

'Please.'

He runs his hand down the length of my body, leaving

a scorching trail in his wake. I squirm beneath him, but he doesn't quicken the pace. In fact, it only seems to make him go slower.

'There's no need to rush, love,' he murmurs as his hands reach my hips. He makes quick work of my skirt before pressing a finger lightly over my still-clothed clit. I jerk my hips forward, desperate for a deeper touch. 'Tell me what you want.'

'You,' I choke out as he slides his hand up and down in languid strokes. 'I want you to touch me. I *need* you to touch me.'

He kisses me softly, swallowing my moan as he tugs down my bikini panties and slides one long finger inside me. My hips buck upwards, but he uses his free hand to hold me in place.

He holds my gaze as he inserts another finger and begins pumping faster than before. 'You're so beautiful, Bailey.'

He says my name with reverence, like it's something worthy of worshipping.

'Stop it,' I mumble.

'No.'

He presses his thumb against my clit. The moan that slips past my lips is low and needy. 'I'll never stop telling you how beautiful you are.'

He brings himself to my eye level, fingers still pumping away, and kisses me. 'How smart you are.'

Another kiss. 'How brilliant you are.'

Another. 'How kind you are.'

Another. 'How *perfect* you are.'

His affirmations make my heart swell, and I'm afraid it might burst. What have I done to deserve such kindness?

Such tenderness?

Such love?

'Cash, I—'

He silences me with another kiss, this one long and deep. When we break apart, he pulls his fingers out of me. I'm about to protest, but he slides down my body and spreads my thighs apart.

'I'm going to taste you now.'

My breath comes out ragged as he flattens his tongue along my opening. I see stars as he sucks my clit and inserts another finger. I reach forward and thread my fingers in his hair, holding his head in a place where the pressure is *just right*.

'Are you gonna come for me, Bailey?'

'*Yes.*'

'Go on then. Do it.' He gives me one long, slow lick. 'Come for me.'

He twists his finger inside me, and I come apart beneath him. I fist my fingers in his hair, my hips lift off the couch, and I cry out his name as I ride this most blissful of waves.

Cash watches me intently as my body shudders and shakes. Once I'm still, he scoops me up in his arms and brings me to our bed.

'You good?' he whispers as he lowers me down, then climbs into the bed with me. He shifts slightly and pulls me over him, so I'm draped across his chest.

'*So* good,' I say with a yawn.

He laughs and gives my shoulder a squeeze. 'I'm glad you enjoyed yourself.'

'Very much so.'

It hits me that I'm the only one who got to properly enjoy our little tryst. I glance down the bed. Cash's dick is straining against the fabric of his shorts. I move to slide down him and release him from the constraints of his clothing, but he holds me firmly in place.

'You're tired.' He kisses my forehead and then peppers a trail of kisses down my face before nipping at my earlobe. 'Trust me, we've got plenty of time to do all the dirty little things running through your mind.'

'You don't know what's running through my mind,' I say stubbornly. 'And I'm not tired.' A yawn that I can't quite stifle escapes me, and I roll my eyes as he laughs at me. 'Maybe just a little.'

Cash pulls me close and kisses me gently. 'Go to sleep, love.'

'Fine. But tomorrow, I'm sucking the hell out of your dick.'

I feel his lips grin against mine.

'It's a date.'

Chapter Fifteen

'You look happy.'

I shrug as I pull a warm, golden dumpling out of the bowl and take a bite. 'We're in Jamaica. The weather's great. What's not to be happy about?'

Across the table from me, Bea and Meera share a pointed look. We're having another girls breakfast morning, although Lacey is nowhere to be seen – thankfully – and Sara has joined the guys in the gym for a quick workout session.

I wonder if it's true what they say and throw a subtle glance at the reflective surface of a nearby spoon to try and see if I'm sporting that so-called *post-sex glow*. Can they tell that Cash and I spent our morning slowly but eagerly exploring each other's bodies? I don't *think* so . . . But my cheeks *are* a little red.

Bea grabs a handful of grapes and pops them into her

mouth. 'You just look happy, that's all,' she says through a mouthful of grapes. 'No need to get defensive.'

Meera nods. 'Happy is *good*. Don't forget that.'

It sounds ridiculous, but in a strange way, I think I need to hear it. It's been so long since I was genuinely happy. I need to force myself to savour the feeling.

Who knows how long it's going to last.

I'm acutely aware of the fact that Cash and I haven't properly discussed the developments that have occurred in our relationship over the last twenty-four hours. There's a horrible voice niggling at the back of my mind, telling me that as soon as we land back in London, everything is going to go right back to normal.

The thought makes me feel sick.

In just a few days, Cash has managed to worm himself into the gaps in my life. And I want him to stay there.

A white mug filled with a dark red liquid slides across the table.

I look up. Cash, Marcus and Sara have returned from the gym. Cash slides into the seat next to me and nods at the mug.

'Some tea,' he says, accurately deciphering the curious expression that flits across my face. 'Berry, right?'

Warmth floods through me, and it's not just because of the sip of tea. 'Perfect.'

I lean towards him, feeling oddly emboldened, and plant

a quick kiss on his cheek. It's the first time I've initiated anything remotely romantic in front of the others, but it feels right.

Nobody comments on it. I remember our first night at the resort, how I'd been so enraptured by how natural and effortless the other couples were with each other. Is that how we look now?

But we're not a real couple.

The thought displeases me more than it should.

'Where're Lacey and Danny?' Sara asks, helping herself to Meera's stack of pancakes.

Lacey's name makes me freeze momentarily. Out of the corner of my eye, I see Cash throw me a look of concern. I give his thigh a squeeze under the table. *I'm all right.*

'Not sure,' says Meera with a shrug. 'I did message her but got no response.'

'Maybe they've gone on an early morning excursion?' says Bea. 'We're doing one tomorrow. We're up at the crack of dawn for a sunrise boat ride.'

Marcus groans. 'Can we cancel? It's way too early.'

'It was *your* idea,' Bea says, deadpan.

'Nah. It was definitely *your* idea.'

We all laugh as Bea and Marcus fall into an easy back and forth, arguing good-naturedly about whose idea it was. I like them together. They're a good couple. It's easy to see where they both support and lift the other up. You can tell they've been together long enough that there are no insecurities there anymore. They slot together like puzzle pieces.

Meera and Sara give off a similar energy, effortlessly bouncing off each other as the conversation pivots, and they share their plans for the day.

'We're going horseback riding,' says Sara through a mouthful of pancake.

Meera slides her a glass of orange juice. 'Sara used to ride as a child.'

'But it's been years since I've tried it,' Sara finishes. She slides the glass back, and Meera takes a sip. 'So we'll see if I've still got it.'

'What about you two?' Meera asks. 'Any plans?'

'We're heading off the resort,' Cash says, grinning widely. 'We're going to check out the local town and spend the day down there.'

'That'll be nice,' says Meera. 'You should check with Penelope and see if she's got any recommendations.'

'Ooh, good idea,' I say.

We finish up our breakfast and then say our farewells, promising to meet up for dinner later that evening. I take Meera's advice and, on the way out of the resort, wave down Penelope.

'We're heading into town. Do you have any recommendations? Places we should check out? Any great restaurants?'

Penelope's eyes light up. She makes me pull out my phone

and open up the notes app, so I can hurriedly jot down all the shops and restaurants and cultural sites she recommends. You can tell she really loves her job. There's an earnest passion that comes through as she tells us all about Sean's Fish Shack ('You *have* to stop there and try the snapper!') or Jeanie's Juices ('Head there for the *best* smoothie of your life!') and tells us which taxi company to go with if we want to head a little further out to visit a nearby market for some handmade souvenirs.

'Actually, are you sure you guys don't want me to call you a car now?' Penelope asks. 'It's about a twenty-minute walk into town from here.'

It's still early enough that the sun isn't at its peak, and the temperature is mild and pleasant. 'I think we'll walk,' I say. 'But thank you, Penelope, for all of this. You've been so helpful.'

'It's my pleasure. Give me a call if you need me.'

We promise that we will and then head off. As soon as we turn away from Penelope, Cash laces our fingers together.

I know such a small action shouldn't make my heart race, but it does. I wonder if his heart is also pumping at a hundred miles an hour right now. He seems so relaxed, so *chill*, like this doesn't bother him at all. As if reaching for my hand and holding me close as we stroll down the dusty road is just second nature to him.

'What're you thinking?'

His quiet murmur startles me, and I peek up at him. He's looking at me with all the intensity of the sun. Like I'm a riddle he can't quite solve.

Why?

The energy between us is so palpable. I can't believe I've never noticed it before. Why is *this* the first time I've allowed myself to get close enough to Cash to feel like this? That horrible voice in the back of my mind returns.

This is just a holiday fling.

Once you're home, he'll never look your way again.

And worst of all . . .

You don't deserve a love like this.

Ethan didn't want you.

And soon, Cash won't either.

'Nothing,' I say brightly, hoping Cash can't see behind my forced smile. We turn a corner, and I can see the town start to crest over the horizon. 'Ready to explore?'

Cash watches me intently, his grey-green eyes narrowing slightly. It's obvious that he doesn't buy it, but he allows me this mercy and doesn't push the topic. Instead, he just shrugs, the intense expression gone from his face and replaced with an easy grin.

'Let's go.'

* * *

Cash has this fascinating ability to charm the pants off everyone we meet. He seems to pick up a new friend at every stall, shop and food truck we pass by.

It's fun watching him talk to the locals, laughing and joking before they inevitably convince him to spend far too much on whatever they're selling.

I don't understand why it's taken me so long to see this side of him. I feel cheated. I've missed out on *years* of this Cash in favour of moody silences and annoyed looks.

Whatever happens between us, I refuse to go back to that dynamic.

'I hope you know you're stuck with me now,' I tell him. We're wandering through the winding town, sipping on frozen fruit smoothies from Jeanie's Juices. Penelope was right. They're delicious.

Cash sips from his mango smoothie and quirks a brow. 'Stuck?'

'Yes, stuck. We're friends for life now. It's a fact. Tell Dane he's got to share you from now on.'

His brows furrow a little bit in what looks like annoyance, but his expression smooths out so quickly I can't be sure. '"*Stuck*" makes it sound like a chore.'

'How would you describe it?'

He pins me in place with a stare that sends heat rippling through me. It's the same look he gave me this morning, and minutes later, my legs were draped over his shoulders. My thighs squeeze together involuntarily.

'I don't know, but I wouldn't use *stuck*,' he says, a stubborn pout twisting his lips. 'Here.' He deftly changes the subject by holding his smoothie out to me. 'Taste.'

I do as he says and can't help the delighted moan that slips from my lips as the ice-cold burst of fruity flavour hits my tongue. 'That's delicious. Try mine.'

I hold my cup up for him to taste, but he bypasses me and instead presses his lips against mine. My mouth opens for him, and his tongue slips in without hesitation. His free hand reaches up to cup my jaw, deepening the kiss.

I don't think I'll ever tire of kissing Cash.

When he moves to pull away, I follow, not ready to end the kiss just yet.

He chuckles and rolls his shoulders back, bringing himself to his full height and out of reach from my lips. 'Yours also tastes delicious.'

'Unfair,' I whisper, letting him lace our fingers together once more so we can continue our stroll. 'I wasn't finished.'

'The day's not over.'

A loud whistle makes us both jump.

'Now *that's* romance!' A cheerful-looking woman sitting behind a makeshift stall hoots at us. There are bundles of colourful flowers set out in front of her. 'Come and finish the job and buy your pretty girlfriend a pretty flower.'

'Oh, we're no—'

Before I can protest, Cash crosses the short distance between the woman and us and plucks a bundle off the stand. He says something to the woman that I can't quite hear. Whatever it is, it makes her smile and glance over at me. She gives Cash an enthusiastic nod and grins widely at me. 'You're a lucky lady.'

Cash walks back to me, an array of colourful flowers in his hands, and I can't help but agree.

He hands me the bouquet with a grin. 'For my lady.'

I give them a tentative sniff. '*Your* lady, huh?'

He shrugs. 'If you'll have me.'

A lump forms in my throat. I grip the stems of the flowers tightly. 'Do you want me?'

He licks his lips. 'I think you know what I want, Bailey.'

I look up at him through my eyelashes and smirk. Memories of our morning spent together beneath the sheets, slowly exploring each other's bodies, flash through my mind. 'Do you want to head back to the suite?'

That almost imperceptible flicker of annoyance is back, and this time it lingers. The mood between us changes almost immediately. It feels like something has wedged itself firmly between us, keeping us at a distance from each other.

'What?' I ask. I lift my free hand to reach for him, then suddenly second-guess myself. I let my arm fall to the side. 'What's wrong?'

He shakes his head. 'Nothing.' His voice is curt and cold. The old Cash is back. He drops my hand and steps away from me. The distance between us widens even further.

'Cash, wait.' I chase after him and grab his hand. 'I'm sorry. I've upset you.'

'You don't have anything to apologise for,' he says quietly. He wraps his arms around me and pulls me flush against his chest, resting his chin on my head. 'We just – We want different things.'

'How do you know what I want?' I ask.

'I just do.'

'I want you,' I tell him. And I do. I want him in my life. However he'll let me. I'll even take scraps if it means I get to keep him in my life for just a little bit longer.

'I know you do.' He pulls back and gives me a sad smile, and I swear his voice cracks a little when he says, 'But not how I want you.'

Chapter Sixteen

My camera roll is full of Cash.

I'm sitting by the pool alone. Ever since yesterday in town, things have changed between Cash and me. He's keeping me at a polite distance, and it feels like we're back to square one. Last night he kept entirely to his side of the bed, and the space between us felt like a never-ending chasm.

I'm getting a horrible sense of déjà vu, only this time, I can't figure out what the problem is.

When he pulled away from me after the cabana bar, I got it. We'd gone too far too fast, and neither of us knew how to reckon with that. But I thought we were on the same page now. That we both wanted the same thing. To indulge in this undeniable attraction that's bloomed between us before the flight back to London brings us back to reality. A reality in which Cash and I are barely acquaintances, just two ships passing in the night.

Our week in paradise is rapidly approaching its end, and the thought makes my stomach twist.

I'm not ready to give this up just yet.

To give *him* up.

I lean back on my sun lounger and scroll through my camera roll. I've asked Penelope, Bea, Meera and Sara to also send me any photos they've snapped of us through the trip, and I'm amazed at how many they've taken. And how happy Cash and I look in all of them.

If I didn't know any better, I'd say that we were a real couple. There's something in our eyes, something about the way we look at each other, that just screams *love*. It shocks me a little to see it reflected in my own eyes. To see how happy and free I look. I don't think I've ever seen this side of myself. Even with Ethan, all our photos were carefully curated to highlight the best parts of our relationship – however few and far between they were.

But there's nothing curated about Cash and me.

These moments are raw, unfiltered, and *real*.

I stop at a photo of Cash and me in town yesterday before everything fell apart. We're standing outside Jeanie's Juices, grinning from ear to ear. Cash has got one arm draped around me, pulling me close to his side. I'm leaning into his chest, smiling like that's my favourite place to be.

I think that it might be, and the thought scares me a little bit.

I choose a handful of photos – none with Cash's face clear in them – and import them into Instagram, adding a quick caption.

FUN TIMES IN JAMAICA AT THE YOU AND I COUPLES RESORT

And then I hit send. For the first time in a while, I don't immediately click out of the app and disconnect from the WiFi. Instead, I watch as the notifications come flooding in. People comment on my outfits, and my hair, and the location, and . . . And there are a few comments about Ethan and Cash too.

@cloudy_mermer12 that's definitely a different guy from The Video. His hair is different.

@kittykatkaty she's got a new boyfriend ALREADY????

@69_qwerty4 DEFO AN UPGRADE. HE'S SO TALL WTF????

@hellohelen934 what kind of guy would willingly date someone like her?

That last comment stings more than any of the others combined. It hits the nail on the head. *Hellohelen934* – almost definitely a burner account for some snotty troll – has asked the question I've been avoiding for the last week.

What kind of person would date someone like me?

Lacey's voice echoes in my mind.

God, you're pathetic.

And it hurts so much because I know it's true.

Maybe it's a good thing that whatever this is between Cash and me, it's not going to survive Jamaica.

We'll go home, and we'll stop being an *us*. There will be no more lingering glances, or soft touches, or fleeting kisses shared in the early hours of the morning. Things will go back to normal, and I can stop pretending like there's ever been a chance that we could be something *more*.

Because there is no chance.

Once Cash finds out the truth, that will be it for us.

I don't realise that I'm crying until a tear splashes against my phone screen.

Chapter Seventeen

There are a million and one things I want to say to Cash right now, but the only thing that comes out is, 'You look *amazing*.'

We're about to head to The Blue Mahoe for our candlelit dinner on the beach. Cash grins at me and gives me a small twirl. He's wearing an olive linen suit that complements his skin tone magnificently. His hair is free from the messy bun he's pulled it in for most of the week, and it falls across his face in soft, luscious-looking waves.

He looks like he's just stepped from the pages of a glossy magazine.

'Then we match,' he says kindly. 'Because you look beautiful.'

'Thank you.' I'm wearing a fitted black dress with an open back. It hugs my curves in all the right places, and I take a tiny bit of pleasure in the glimpse of heat I see behind his eyes as he checks me out.

Maybe all isn't lost.

'Do you want to take a photo?' I ask.

'Sure.' He reaches his hand out to take my phone, but I shake my head.

'No, not of *me*.' I take a step towards him, ignoring the thudding sensation in my chest. 'Together. Do you want to take a photo of us together?'

His eyes widen a fraction. We've taken plenty of photos together throughout the trip, but they've mostly been in front of the others. Part of the façade of our loving relationship. Cash suggested the photo we took at Jeanie's Juices, but this is the first time I've asked for a photo when it's just been the two of us.

I would give anything to be able to hear the marathon of thoughts currently racing through his mind as he stares at me. There's a conflict raging behind his eyes, and I wonder which way he's going to land.

I take another step forwards, making my intentions known.

We only have two days left in Jamaica, and I'm going to push for this.

I'm going to push for us.

'Cash?'

'Sure.' His voice sounds like sandpaper. 'How – How do you want me?'

On the bed, laid out in front of me, my thighs wrapped around your waist.

Instead, I say, 'Over here is fine.'

I place my phone on the coffee table and set a timer on the camera app. I pull Cash towards the sliding doors, where the backdrop of the Jamaican sunset is casting our suite and the surroundings outside in an ethereal glow.

He slides an arm around my waist, and I press my hand against his chest. I can feel his heartbeat pumping against my palm.

'It'll take a few,' I tell him.

He nods, and we pose as my phone fires off a rapid burst of photos. His hand squeezes my waist, and I look up at him. He's looking down at me, that recognisable fire in his eyes.

He wants this. I know he does. Why is he depriving himself?

'Bailey,' he whispers, and why have I never noticed just how good my name sounds coming from him?

I tilt my head up, eyes fluttering shut. *Go on*, I silently urge. *Do it. Kiss me.*

He doesn't.

The sound of my camera shutter stops abruptly, plunging us into silence.

He takes a step away from me, his hand dropping from my waist as he turns away. 'We should go. Don't want to be late for dinner.'

'Right,' I say. The rejection chokes in my throat. 'Let's go.'

★ ★ ★

Penelope leads our group out to the back of The Blue Mahoe, where the doors open out to the beach. We turn a corner and see a secluded area with four small gazebos, each a short distance away from the nearest one, providing an air of privacy. The gazebos are covered with soft, billowing white curtains with a floral pattern across them. Beneath each gazebo is a small table and two comfortable-looking chairs. There's a candle on each table, illuminating the scene.

'Please, have a seat!' Penelope says to us all with a wide grin. 'Dinner will be served shortly.'

Cash wordlessly holds out his hand to help me navigate the sand in my heels. Things may be awkward between us currently, but he's still a gentleman. I grip his forearm to steady myself as we walk towards our gazebo.

Irritatingly, Lacey and Danny are seated in the gazebo closest to ours. I've managed to avoid her for the most part ever since that day by the pool, but she catches my eye as we all hobble across the sand.

'Careful, Bea,' she calls with a sneer. 'The sand is really uneven. You don't want Bailey to trip and steal your man.'

Anger crashes down on me like waves against the shore. I choke down the venom-laced words I desperately want to hurl back at her and force myself to keep looking forward. I don't even glance back to see how the others have reacted. I won't give her the attention she wants.

'What is her problem?' Cash murmurs. It's the first thing

he's said directly to me since we left the suite. His grip on my hand tightens slightly. It's a small comfort.

'Ignore her,' I say. 'Just ignore her.'

Cash makes an irritated sound but doesn't say anything else. He leads me to our gazebo and pulls my chair out. I drop it into it and realise, with a twinge of annoyance, that I can see Lacey perfectly from here.

She raises a perfectly plucked brow at me, then turns to Danny and says, 'I just don't think I'd ever be able to trust a cheater.' She's acting like she's only talking to him, and they're resuming a conversation they've already begun, but her voice is loud enough to carry over the waves and reach the others in their gazebos.

She's goading me, and Cash can tell too.

'Can you *stop*?' Cash says sharply, raising his voice, so there's no mistaking who he's talking to.

Danny shifts in his seat and fixes Cash with a stern look. 'You watch how you talk to my lady.'

'It's *fine*,' I say through gritted teeth. 'Don't worry about it.'

Cash shoots both Lacey and Danny a withering glare before he turns his attention back to me. 'It's clearly not fine.'

I'm saved from having to respond as a waiter approaches to pour wine into our glasses and recite tonight's menu.

'Chef Pépin has three phenomenal mains on offer tonight.

Traditional Jamaican curry goat; rum glazed pork tenderloin; or lobster sautéed in coconut milk.'

They all sound delicious, but there's a knot of anxiety forming in my stomach that's rapidly erasing any appetite I may have had. I opt for lobster, and Cash goes for the curry goat. The waiter gives us a polite nod and then disappears back into the restaurant to fulfil our order.

Once he's gone, the silence between us seems to stretch on for an eternity. It doesn't help that all around us, I can hear Bea and Marcus giggling softly or that I can see Meera and Sara staring lovingly into each other's eyes. Even Lacey and Danny look happy, a picture of perfection as Lacey snaps photos and videos of the waves crashing onto the beach.

When the waiter comes back with our dishes, we've still not said a word.

My heart hurts as I watch him slice into his meal, deliberately avoiding making any eye contact with me.

'How is it?' I ask quietly. My voice is wobbly, and I realise I'm on the verge of tears.

'It's great,' he mumbles, still not looking up from his plate. 'And yours?'

'*Cash.*'

There must be something in my voice because, this time, he looks up. His eyes are dark and haunted.

'Talk to me,' I plead. 'I don't want to . . . I don't want to lose you. Not like this.'

'I'm not going anywhere.'

'You know what I mean.'

Lacey's high-pitched laughter trills over to us, and I feel myself stiffen at the sound.

Cash puts his knife and fork down and pins me down with a sharp look. 'What's going on with you two?'

'Nothing,' I lie.

'I'm not an idiot, Bailey,' he says.

'I didn't say you were.'

'You're treating me like I am one.'

'And you're treating me like I'm *nothing*.' I spit the last word out like it's acid on my tongue. 'How do you think that makes me feel?'

'You could never be nothing to me,' Cash says quietly.

'Let's be honest with each other,' I say.

Cash leans back in his chair, runs a hand down his face, and groans. Then he looks me square in the eye and says, 'You first.'

'I—' I pause and swallow. He's right. I've not been honest with him. I've been withholding so much out of fear. But we've reached the tipping point now, and I know what I need to do.

'I went back to him,' I say as quickly as I can, desperate to get the words out before I change my mind. 'Ethan. I went back to Ethan. Even after I found out about his girlfriend, I still went back to him. I wanted him to choose *me*.' My breath comes out in ragged gulps, and my vision blurs with tears. I can't believe I'm telling him this. 'I wanted him to apologise and to say I was the one he really wanted.'

Cash slides a napkin across the table, and I dab it against my eyes.

'You know, he didn't defend me even once. He just sat there and let her throw wine over me and hurl abuse at me. He let me take all the blame when *none* of it was my fault. And even after everything he put me through, I still wanted him. I went to his house and tried to get him to take me back. Can you believe that?' Now I have started talking, I can't stop. The words pour from my mouth without reprieve. 'And how could I not know that he was cheating on me for two years? The signs were all there. I think I did know, subconsciously. I just didn't want to admit it because I'm what? So desperate for love that I'll look the other way just to be in a relationship? With someone like *him*. I'm *pathetic*.'

'You're not pathetic, Bailey.'

'But I *am*. Lacey can see it. Everyone online can see it. Why can't *you*?' The tears are falling freely now – napkin be damned. 'You talk about me like I'm this . . . this perfect being, when I'm not. I'm a mess. A pathetic mess. Why can't you see that?'

'You're not a mess,' Cash says quietly. He reaches across the table and gives my hand a squeeze. 'And Ethan was – *is* – an asshole. He didn't deserve you, and you're not any less of a person for wanting to be loved. You deserve someone who's going to love you without you having to fight for it. You deserve someone who's going to make you their priority.'

'I don't deserve someone like that.'

'Why not?'

The question hangs between us like a weight.

When I don't respond, Cash pushes me. 'Why not, Bailey? Tell me why you don't deserve that?'

I open my mouth, an answer on the tip of my tongue, but nothing comes out. I don't know how to articulate this maelstrom of thoughts that have been swirling in my mind ever since I found out about Ethan and his girlfriend.

How can I explain to him that Ethan has single-handedly shattered every smidgen of confidence in myself I ever possessed? That I look in the mirror and see a pathetic, desperate husk of my former self blinking back at me?

Cash squeezes my hand to get my attention. 'You do deserve it, Bailey. And I'll tell you that every day for the rest of our lives if that's what it takes for you to never feel like this again.'

My breath hitches in my throat. 'For the rest of our—'

'Bailey, I fucking love you,' Cash says, the words spilling out of his mouth like they've been waiting on the tip of his tongue for too long. 'I love you, and I want to show you the kind of love you deserve. If you'll let me.'

I blink at him. 'No, you don't.'

'I do,' he says simply. 'I've loved you since we were teenagers.'

'*Why?*' I croak.

'Why not? I keep telling you, you're amazing. You're beautiful, smart, driven, kind. You make me feel like a better person just being in the same room as you.'

The world is spinning around me. Cash loves me.

Cash *loves* me.

Cash loves *me*.

'But you didn't even *like* me until this trip,' I protest. I can't wrap my head around it. Cash is attracted to me. Yes, that's obvious. But love?

Love?

He grimaces and looks down for a moment. 'I never thought we'd ever have a chance to be together, so I kept you at a distance. I thought that would help dull my feelings a little bit, but it never worked. That dinner at your parents' house the week before we flew out?'

I remember it well, particularly how irritated he seemed to be with my presence.

'That was my own personal hell,' he admits with a wry grin. 'Seeing you like that, because of *Ethan* of all people—' He shakes his head. 'I wanted to jump across the table, pull you into my arms and never let go. I wanted to tell you then and there that someone like him doesn't deserve your tears.'

'Cash, I—'

'I don't need you to say it back to me, Bailey. I know you don't love me and that this is just a holiday fling for you, but for me, it's not.'

'Is that why you got so quiet yesterday?' I ask, remembering how the mood had changed so abruptly between us when I suggested heading back to the suite. 'And why you didn't want to continue with anything that first night?'

He nods. 'I thought that maybe you were falling for me too. But then I realised it was just sex for you. I thought that I could handle it and that I'd just be grateful to have this time with you. But I can't do it. Not without you knowing how I feel.'

'It's not just the sex for me,' I whisper. His eyes widen, and he swallows thickly. 'I thought it was after that first night. That you were just an itch I needed to scratch. But it's not. There's something here between us.' I place my free hand over his and give it a small squeeze. 'I feel it. It might not be love yet for me, but—' I inhale deeply and force myself to meet his gaze. 'I want us to get there.'

Pure happiness blooms across his face. 'We'll get there.' He says it like it's an immutable fact. Like there's no doubt in his mind that one day – one day *soon* – I'll have caught up with him, and we'll both be wildly in love with the other.

I nod in agreement. 'We will.'

'I will never hurt you, Bailey,' he says. 'Not like Ethan. Not like anyone. You can trust me. Let me in. Let me love you the way you deserve to be loved. Let me show you how love should feel.'

I take a deep breath and offer him a watery smile. 'Okay.'

Chapter Eighteen

Cash's hand is snaking up my thigh before the door to our suite swings closed.

I moan as his mouth catches mine, and I return each frenzied caress of his tongue with equal eagerness. His hands squeeze the top of my thighs and move to cup the soft curve of my ass. I huff out a startled squeak as he presses his thigh between my legs, using at leverage as he hoists me up and pins me against the wall. I wrap my legs around him immediately, my arms and legs working overtime to pull him as close to me as he can possibly get.

He tears his lips away from mine and, breathing heavily, rests his forehead against mine. For a moment, time seems to stop. It's just him and me in this dark suite.

'*Fuck*, Bailey,' he groans, voice low and gravelly. '*Fuck*.'

I giggle through my own panted breaths. 'Very eloquent.'

He laughs, and the sound sends reverberations through my chest. 'I can't think straight.'

'So don't think,' I whisper against his lips. 'Just do.'

He nods, then pulls me away from the wall, tightening his hold on me. I keep our gazes locked as he carries me across the suite. I don't want to miss a single second of this. His knees bump against the edge of the bed, and he lowers me down onto it. As soon as my back hits the soft mattress, I swivel around, reaching for the zip of my dress, but Cash grabs my hand and holds me still.

He's hovering over me, his dick straining against the linen fabric of his trousers, a hungry look in his eyes.

I lick my lips and enjoy the way his eyes follow the wet trail I make along my lower lip.

'Stop stalling,' I murmur as I try to wriggle free from his grasp and grip the zip of my dress.

He kneels on the mattress, pushing me further into it. 'I'm not stalling. I just—' He pulls my hand to the front and holds it firmly in place. 'Keep the dress on.' His voice comes out as a rough keen. '*Please.*'

I raise a brow. 'This is an expensive dress.'

'It'll come off eventually,' he promises, bringing his face down to meet mine. 'But let me savour you in it for a little longer.'

I lift my head and capture his lower lip between my bottom teeth. I hear a sharp inhale and then a low groan as I suck on his lip. His obvious pleasure spurs me on. I pull away from him, biting back a smirk when he huffs in irritation at the sudden absence of my lips on his.

I wrap my legs around his waist and angle my body to the side. 'Lie down.'

His eyebrows shoot into his hairline. 'Huh?'

I give him a firm shake, disorienting him enough that he leans to the side enough for me to push him all the way. I roll him onto his back and sit up, straddling his waist.

There's a look of reverence in his eyes as he looks at me through hooded lids. His hands run up and down my bare thighs, and his touch sends liquid fire running through my veins.

I let him savour the moment for a long minute, enjoying the way his hips have begun to involuntarily buck upwards into mine. Then I lift myself off him, and I relish in the look of frustration that flashes across his face.

'Someone's impatient,' I say as I stand upright, watching his chest heave as he takes deep breaths.

'*Someone's* a tease.'

'Fair. But I thought you wanted to see me in this dress.'

He swallows, his Adam's apple bobbing in his throat. 'I do.'

'Then let me show you.'

He sits up as I step back so he can get a full view of my body. I run my hands down the front of my dress, stopping only briefly at my breasts. His breath hitches as my fingers ghost over my nipples.

'*Bailey.*'

'Tell me how I look in this dress,' I tell him, the order slipping from my lips with surprising ease. 'Tell me how badly you want me.'

Something hot flashes in his eyes, and his dick stirs in his trousers. 'I don't have the words to explain how badly I want you, Bailey. You're driving me crazy. I—' He reaches a hand out to me, but I smack it away.

'Wait.' I look him up and down and shake my head. 'You're wearing entirely too much. Take it off.'

'Take what off?'

'Everything.'

He doesn't hesitate. The speed at which he sheds his blazer and pops the buttons of his shirt is impressive. Guinness World Record levels of speed. He throws his blazer and shirt into a dark corner of the room and then moves to unbuckle his belt.

'Wait,' I say again, my lips curling as he fixes me with a look that oozes frustration. 'Let me.' I lean over him and brush my fingers against the metal of his belt. He holds his breath as I ease the leather strip out of the metal and pull it free from the loops around his waist. Once the belt isn't in the way anymore, he makes quick work of his trousers, and then he's sitting on the bed, legs spread wide, in only his boxers.

'Is that painful?' I ask, nodding to his crotch, where his dick strains against the light fabric of his boxers.

'In the best kind of way.'

I match his grin and continue ghosting my hands over my still-clothed body. The way he looks at me makes me feel bolder and sexier than I ever have before. 'Touch yourself while you tell me what you want to do to me,' I instruct.

His hand immediately dives into his boxers, pulling his dick free from its fabric prison. I try not to gawk at it, but, judging by the way he smirks, I fail.

His hands slowly begin to pump up and down his length, his thumb making small circles over the head, swirling over the precum that's already begun to drip down.

'Tell me,' I say, my voice barely above a whisper. 'Tell me what you want.'

He doesn't break eye contact or stop pumping his hand as he begins. 'I want you. I want you in every way imaginable.'

'You'll need to be more specific than that,' I say as I spin on the spot, showing off the expanse of back my dress puts on a show. 'Where do you want me?'

'Right here,' he groans, using his free hand to point at his dick. 'As soon as we're finished here, I want you to sit on it. Can you do that for me, baby? Can you sit on my dick?'

I wonder if he notices the way *baby* slips out or if he notices the way it makes me squirm.

'I can do that.'

'You look so beautiful in that dress,' he says, gaze still firmly locked onto mine. 'You look beautiful in everything, but that dress . . .' He groans loudly, his hips bucking slightly. 'Bailey, I don't want to finish like this.'

'How do you want to finish?'

'Inside you.'

I reach my hand behind me and feel for the zip of my dress. In one smooth move, I tug the zip downwards, and my dress falls to the ground. Cash's hand stills on his dick.

'*Fucking hell.*'

I kick off my heels and saunter slowly towards the bed, edging his thighs apart with my knee as I approach.

'Bailey . . .' he says, his voice a warning I don't intend to heed.

I straddle his waist, the thin layer of my panties acting as the only thing between his dick and my pulsating pussy. He brings his hands up to cup my breasts. His thumb runs over my nipple, and I can't help but gasp at the touch.

We've explored each other's bodies already, but this feels new. Like now that there's nothing between us – no lies, no half-truths – we're able to fully give ourselves to one another. And Cash doesn't hold back.

He runs his thumbs over my nipples again, gently plucking at the buds as they stiffen and harden. 'I'm never going to get tired of this.'

'Me neither,' I say.

He leans forward, presses his tongue flat against my nipple, and sucks it gently, experimentally. My keening whine clearly gives him the confidence to keep going because he suddenly bites down, and I throw my head back and cry out his name.

'You like biting,' he murmurs against my breasts. 'Noted.'

I thread my fingers through his hair and pull his head up to meet mine. 'I think I just like *you*.'

He gives me a lopsided smirk. 'Also noted.'

He drops his hands from my breasts and slides them down my sides. I shiver at the touch. He's being so gentle, like he's mapping out every inch of my body and committing it to memory as he goes. His fingers tug at the thin material sitting low on my hips.

Grey-green eyes meet mine, and I give him a nod.

He grins, wide and bright, and then yanks my panties down. I lift myself slightly in his lap so I can pull them off. As soon they're gone, joining the rest of his clothes in a dark corner of the room, Cash presses a finger against my clit.

'Oh, *fuck me*,' I cry, curving my back, so my breasts brush against his chest.

'That's the plan,' Cash murmurs. He finds my lips again and pulls me into another searing kiss. He slides his finger up and down my soaking pussy, and I squirm irritably on his lap.

'Enough,' I whisper into his ear. 'I'm ready.'

He doesn't need to be told twice. He lifts me slightly, adjusts himself, and then pulls me down on his dick. I throw my head back and moan his name so loudly I'm scared our neighbours might hear.

'Yes, baby,' Cash murmurs in my ear. He's shaking slightly as he forces himself to stay still and not move, giving me time to adjust to his size and make myself comfortable. 'You'll tell me if it's too much?'

'It's not,' I pant, experimentally rolling my hips.

The groan he emits is out of this world. He's looking at me like I'm a work of art – his *favourite* piece of art. He brings his hand to cup my ass cheeks and roughly squeezes them, helping to bounce me as I rock my hips back and forth.

We fall into an easy rhythm. Cash bucks upwards when I drop down onto him, creating a pleasurable kind of dance. The sounds he's making are like a sweet melody composed just for me. I don't think I'll ever tire of hearing him moan my name or the way words like *baby* and *sweetheart* and *love* fall from his lips as he heaps me with praise.

Listen to him tell it, and I'm the best he's ever had.

That shot to the ego is what sends me overboard.

'*God, Bailey.* You feel so *fucking good.*'

And then I'm crashing into him, crying out his name as the force of my orgasm brings me to the brink of tears.

He runs his hands up and down my bare back and whispers in my ear. 'Let me fuck you, Bailey.'

I nod into his chest and swallow my squeak of surprise when he suddenly flips us over, so I'm lying on my back, looking up at him. I barely have the chance to shoot him a quizzical look before he kisses me, hard and deep, and slides back inside me. Just as hard. Just as deep.

I cross my legs at the ankles against his back, pulling him as close as we can possibly get.

'*Shit*,' he half collapses against me, one hand holding him up to stop his weight from squashing mine entirely. 'Bailey, this is – You feel – I can't—' He leans down and drags his teeth along the length of my throat, biting down once he reaches my collarbone. 'Can I – inside?'

'Yes,' I pant. 'I'm on the pill. You can come inside. Please. Please, baby.'

He groans into my neck and lets himself come undone. With one final moan of my name, he shudders and bucks into me one last time before he stills and collapses on top of me.

The only sound in our room is our panted breaths, mixing together to make one. He rolls off me, chest heaving as he rides out the final wave of his orgasm.

'That was—'

'Yeah,' I say.

'Are you okay?' he asks, and I'm sure I hear a hint of nervousness in his tone.

I roll over onto my side and curl up against his chest. He immediately wraps his arm around me and pulls me close so my head is resting just above his heartbeat. The rhythmic thudding is comforting.

'I'm more than okay,' I tell him.

He tips my chin up with a finger and presses a soft kiss against my lips. 'I love you, Bailey. And I'm not saying that to pressure you into saying it back. I'm saying it because it's true, and I've wanted to say it for so long, and now that I can, I don't think I'm ever going to stop.'

I smile against his lips. 'You'll wait for me to get there?' Because I know I'm going to. It's only a matter of time.

'I'll wait for as long as you need.'

For some reason, I don't think he'll be waiting for long.

★ ★ ★

After we clean up, shower, and crawl back into bed together, something suddenly hits me.

'Oh God,' I say. 'Dane is going to lose his mind.'

Cash snorts. 'He probably won't be as surprised as you might think.'

I frown up at him. 'Have you – You haven't *told* him yet, have you?' I'm suddenly paralysed with fear that Cash has been secretly informing Dane about everything that's gone on between us during the trip. Dane and I are relatively close for siblings, but we're not *that* close. The last thing I want my brother to know is the intricacies of my sex life with his best friend.

'I haven't told him anything,' he says, running a reassuring hand down my arm. 'But . . .' He trails off, and when I look up at him, the tips of his ears are pink.

'What?' I ask.

'He knows that I have feelings for you,' Cash says quickly, the pink on his ears rapidly spreading to his cheeks. 'He's known for a while now.'

I remember the way Dane roared with laughter when I told him how I thought Cash didn't like me. This whole trip, in fact, had been Dane's idea.

Realisation slowly dawns on me.

'Did – Did *Dane* set us up?'

Cash runs a nervous hand through his hair. 'Kind of. He, uh, he said he was tired of watching me pine over you. I don't think he thought that *this* would happen, though. Maybe that we'd just get to know each other a little more.'

'Has Dane *always* known?' I ask. 'Like, since we were teenagers?'

Cash nods. 'It's actually his fault I never asked you out.'

'How do you mean?'

'I told him that I liked you when we were about fifteen, I think, and he wasn't happy.' He pulls a face as he pulls the memory to the forefront of his mind. 'Said you were off limits and I'd be a bad friend if I pursued anything with you.'

'I don't know why, but I feel offended,' I laugh. Dane has never really slipped into the 'overprotective big brother' role for me, so it's weird to hear this. It's not something I'd expect from him.

Cash shrugs. 'He was really serious about it as well, so I never said anything. I thought that maybe the feelings would go away, but they didn't. Every time I saw you or even heard anything about you, it was like I was being handed another fifty reasons to love you. I tried moving on. Dated other people.' He grimaces again, like he's remembering something particularly painful. 'But you've always been there in the back of my mind. Quietly driving me crazy.'

'So what changed?' I asked. 'Why did Dane suddenly change his mind and give you his blessing?'

'We were just talking one night, reminiscing about the past, and he remembered that I "used" to have a crush on you.' A soft smile tugs at the corners of his lips. I wish I could see the memory that's currently playing out in his mind. 'And I guess he could tell from my reaction that I still had feelings. Can you believe he actually asked me why I've never tried anything with you?'

'He's the one who told you not to!'

'Exactly,' Cash laughs, shaking his head slightly. 'But he says he doesn't remember ever saying that. Said it was just him being a stupid teenager and that, if I ever got the chance, I should take it.'

I lay back down, resting my head against his chest. 'I'm glad you did.'

'Me too.'

Chapter Nineteen

It's our last full day in Jamaica, and we're spending it together as a group. Penelope has organised a bamboo rafting experience along a nearby river.

We'll spend the afternoon navigating our rafts down a three-mile stretch of river before heading to a nearby village for lunch. I'm excited to get off the resort one last time, but I'm mostly excited to spend the day with Cash as a *real* couple. For the first time since we arrived in Jamaica, our relationship isn't a façade.

I'm so excited to finally spend one day on this trip the way it was intended. I don't even mind when I arrive in the lobby to find that Lacey and Danny are the only people waiting there.

I've come down early, leaving Cash back in the suite to finish up in the shower, hoping to spot Penelope to ask if there's any chance Cash and I can get a last-minute reservation at The Blue Mahoe this evening. Last night, as revelatory as it was, wasn't exactly the height of romance, and I'd like a redo. I want Cash and me to have a happy memory in Jamaica that doesn't end with me in tears or us awkwardly avoiding each other for days.

But Penelope's not there.

Lacey looks up at me as I approach. Her lips curl into a sneer when I drop into the empty seat next to her. I can't bring myself to care.

Cash knows the truth now, and I have nothing to hide. Lacey has no power over me anymore.

'I'm impressed, Bailey.'

I glance over at her. We've been sitting in silence for the last few minutes, and I hadn't expected her to break it. 'What's that?'

'I said, I'm *impressed*.'

'Impressed with what?' I ask, deciding to take the bait if only to end whatever the hell this is. My gaze slides to Danny, and he gives me an imperceptible shrug as if to say he has no idea what's going on either.

Lacey looks ridiculously pleased with herself as she brandishes her phone in front of me. 'You certainly have a type, don't you?'

'I have no idea what you're talking about.'

The sound of sandals slapping against the cold tile flooring snatches my attention away from Lacey.

'*Bailey!*' Sara sings my name as she steps, arm in arm with Meera, into the lobby. They're followed by Bea and Marcus, who both give me a wave when they spot me.

'Hey, girl.' Bea leans down and pulls me into a one-armed hug. 'You look great.'

I beam up at her. After this trip, I'm determined to make sure I stay in contact with Bea, Meera and Sara. 'Thanks. You do too.'

'Where's Cash?' Meera asks as they all drop into the empty chairs around us.

'He's just—'

'He's probably on the phone with his *girlfriend.*'

My head snaps up so fast. I'm surprised my neck doesn't snap. Everyone stares at Lacey, identical looks of confusion mirrored across our faces. Even Danny looks uneasy, like he's not entirely on board with whatever Lacey has planned.

I don't know what's going on either, but I know I don't like it. 'What the hell are you talking about?' I ask.

'Stop playing dumb,' Lacey says with a roll of her eyes. 'I'm sick of it. This good girl act you've been playing this entire holiday.' When nobody responds, she waves her phone wildly in front of her. 'How am *I* the only one who sees this? She's a fucking fraud.'

Does she know? That Cash and I have been faking our relationship this entire time? But how?

'*Lace,*' Danny says sharply.

'No, babe, I'm sick of it! She's a dirty little liar, and she's got you all wrapped around her finger!'

'*Lacey*, chill!' Bea says. She shoots Lacey a ferocious glare that sends a cold shiver down my spine. Remind me never to get on Bea's bad side. 'I don't know what you're talking about, but you're doing entirely too much.'

'Yeah,' says Meera. 'Whatever your problem with Bailey is—'

'My problem is that she's a fucking cheater.'

'Again with this?' I snap, finally reaching my limit. 'I already told you; Ethan was cheating on *me* too. I didn't know what was going on. I don't care if you believe me or not. That's the truth.'

'But it's not the truth, is it?' Lacey snarls. 'If that were the truth, you wouldn't have tried to crawl back to him, would you?'

I stiffen slightly but hold my ground. 'I don't have to explain myself to you.'

'Why do you even care?' asks Bea.

'Because I'm sick of girls like her!' Lacey jabs a finger in my direction. 'They have no sense of loyalty to other women. They have *no* respect for themselves or the relationship they're destroying.'

'*I* didn't destroy anyone's relationship. Ethan did that all by himself.'

'And what about Cash's relationship?' Lacey sneers. 'What

about his girlfriend? I suppose you're innocent in this one too?'

'*I'm* Cash's girlfriend!'

She brandishes her phone again, and this time I can see what's on her screen. It's Cash's Instagram page. The name *@CASHMONEY93* jumps out at me, and I easily recognise the only two posts on his page.

'What—'

Lacey taps on the 'tagged pictures' tab, and the page suddenly fills with rows and rows of photos.

My heart stops for a second or two.

'No,' Lacey says slowly, carefully. '*This* is Cash's girlfriend. Her name is Naomi, and by the looks of it, they've been together for about six months.'

I snatch Lacey's phone from her hand and frantically tap through the photos. She's right. There are almost six months' worth of posts from someone called *@naomi_xoxo* in Cash's 'tagged pictures' tab. He's not in all of them. Some of the photos are of fancy-looking plates, clearly taken on date nights, and Cash has been tagged as a knife or fork. But there are plenty of photos of *them*.

My stomach twists as I land on a photo of them together at a party. She – *Naomi* – is curled up on Cash's lap, leaning into his chest, with a soft smile on her face. Cash's arm is wrapped around her waist, hand resting on her upper thigh.

I look at the post date.

Three weeks ago.

Bile rises in my throat. Lacey says something, but I don't hear. I can't hear anything except for the sound of my own thudding heart.

God. Is there something wrong with me? Something fundamentally wrong about me that makes me only attractive to men like this? Is this my future? My destiny? Always the side piece, never the *one*?

My vision blurs, and I stumble against the wall. This cannot be happening to me again. Not with Cash, of all people. It can't.

I can hear the muffled sounds of Bea and Sara jumping to defend me, but I can't bring myself to respond. My heartbeat quickens even more, and I clutch at the wall behind me. It's getting harder to breathe. Each breath that manages to come out is shallower than the one before. I take several large, gulping breaths, hand pressed tightly against my chest as I try to coax some air into my lungs. It doesn't work.

All I can hear is blood rushing through my veins as I struggle to breathe. My chest feels tight, and my legs begin to buckle.

I can't do this. It's too much. I can—

'Bailey,' Cash says.

For one long moment, everything around me seems to

freeze. Lacey's yelling quietens to a muted whisper, my heartbeat slows down, and I can breathe again.

Cash is standing by my side, one arm wrapped protectively around my shoulders, squeezing lightly as his thumb rubs soothing circles over my collarbone. His brows are knit together with worry, and I can see the question already forming on the tip of his tongue.

I lock eyes with him and remember what he told me last night.

I will never hurt you, Bailey.
Not like Ethan.
Not like anyone.
You can trust me.

I take a deep breath and collapse into his embrace. I bury my face in his chest, relishing the way his strong arms come up to circle me in a tight hug, and I decide that he's right.

I *can* trust him. And we need to talk.

Before anyone else has the chance to speak, I lunge for Cash's arm and drag him away down a small, dark corridor. As we disappear from their sight, I hear Lacey starting up again, trying to convince the others that I'm the evil slut she's made me out to be in her mind.

'Bailey?' Cash asks, worry tinging his tone. 'What's happened?'

I wait till I'm sure we're out of eavesdropping distance from the others, then grind to a halt and turn and face him. I cross my arms over my chest and try to steady my breathing.

'Who's Naomi?'

Several emotions flurry across Cash's face. Surprise. Worry. Anger. Irritation. He settles on a weird mix between surprised and irritated.

'She's my ex,' he says tentatively. 'Why?'

I feel a small bit of relief at how readily he gives up that information. I'd half been expecting him to deny any knowledge of the name. 'Lacey seems pretty sure that she's your girlfriend. Your *real* girlfriend.'

Irritation morphs into anger. His face twists into an uncharacteristic scowl, and he glances over his shoulder as if he expects Lacey to be behind him, sneering at us. '*What?*'

I tell him what just happened with Lacey before he arrived, and I watch as the anger on his face melts into panic. He takes a step closer to me, grabs my hands and presses them against his chest.

'I would never do that to you.'

That tightness in my chest eases up.

'I *won't* ever do that to you.'

'I know,' I whisper. And it's the truth. I know down in the deepest parts of my soul that Cash would never hurt me like Ethan did. 'But why was she posting you only three weeks ago?'

Cash sighs. 'I didn't know that she was still posting. I told you I don't use Instagram very often. I mainly just kept it to check in on you every now and then. You know, as the leader of your fan base and all that.'

I laugh, and the sound seems to cut through some of the tension that's been building. I immediately feel a little lighter, and he can't help but crack a smile too.

'We broke up about two months ago. It wasn't . . . amicable.' He pulls a face, and suddenly the grimace from last night when he mentioned dating other people makes sense. 'She still wants us to get back together, but it's not happening. I've got her blocked on my phone, and I guess that's why she's still tagging me in things on Instagram. She's still trying to get my attention somehow.'

'Why'd you break up?'

'It was a toxic relationship. Let's just put it that way.'

I can tell he doesn't want to say any more – not yet anyway – and I don't push. I know all about toxic relationships, and I know he'll tell me when he's ready.

'I swear, Bailey, that's the truth. You can even ask Dane. He'll tell you.'

I hold up my hand to stop him. 'I trust you, Cash. I just needed to hear it from you.' I lace our fingers together and give him a little squeeze.

He pulls me into a long hug, burying his face in my hair. When we eventually pull apart, his signature sunshine smile is back. 'You're my world, Bailey,' he murmurs. 'I hope you know that.'

My heart feels like it's about seven sizes too big for my chest. I don't know what I've done to deserve Cash and his love, but I'm going to hold onto him for as long as I possibly can.

Chapter Twenty

We return to the lobby, hand in hand, bracing ourselves for another onslaught of verbal abuse from Lacey. But when we get there, Lacey and Danny are nowhere in sight.

Penelope is there now, nervously chewing her bottom lip as she frantically stabs at her iPad. When she spots Cash and me, her eyes go wide, and she hurries across the floor to meet us in the middle.

'Bailey. Cash. I am *so* sorry about everything that just happened.'

I shake my head. 'Penelope, it's fine. This has nothing to do with you or the resort. Don't worry about it.'

Penelope speaks at a million miles an hour. 'No, but I'm supposed to be taking care of you and making sure you're having a good time. I've noticed that she's been a little off with you these last few days, but I didn't want to say anything or pry, but I should have.'

'It's *fine*,' I say, a little more firmly now. I glance around the lobby, half expecting Lacey to be lurking behind a large potted plant. 'Where are they?'

'They're going to spend the day enjoying the resort,' says Penelope through slightly gritted teeth. 'I cannot tolerate a guest treating another guest like that. Not under my care. It's just not right. Whatever issues you have between you two, we expect our guests to remain civil with one another. We'll keep you separate for the rest of the trip. You won't have to worry about her anymore. Now, are you ready to put all this behind you and enjoy the day we've got planned?'

We both nod, and Penelope guides us to the rest of the group. Cash keeps his arm firmly around my shoulders, his lips twisted into an uncharacteristic frown. His entire demeanour is a subtle warning to the others, but it's unnecessary.

As soon as we approach, Sara launches herself into my arms and gives me a hug.

'Are you okay?' she asks. 'That was *horrible*, Bailey. So horrible. I don't know what got into her.'

'She got even worse after you guys left,' says Meera. She shakes her head in disgust. 'I think it really bothered her that we all didn't immediately jump on the Bailey Hate Train with her.'

'Well, why would we?' Bea scoffs. She waves a hand at Cash. 'Anyone with eyes can see that this idiot is madly in love with you. The Instagram stuff was weird, yeah, but we knew there had to be an explanation.' She glances pointedly at Cash's arm, still holding me tightly, and the way I'm leaning into his chest, and smiles. 'And it seems like there was.'

I look between Bea, Meera and Sara and feel tears begin to pool. Outside of my friendship with Amber, I don't think I've ever felt such a warm sense of camaraderie before. It's beautiful.

I'm suddenly struck with the knowledge that I'm leaving Jamaica with more than one new relationship.

Bea swings her legs up and pushes herself out of her seat. 'Now, let's go and do some rafting.'

★ ★ ★

'We need to go on a date.'

We're back in our suite after a truly amazing day of bamboo rafting down the river. We were both fully able to enjoy the day without the pressure and anxiety that comes with having to fake a relationship, and we've made memories that will last a lifetime. My camera roll is nothing but smiling faces and videos filled with laughter and shrieking. I can't wait to pull them all together into a vlog once we get back home.

The only downside of the day is when Bea and I get a quiet moment to ourselves, and I finally discover why Lacey was so hell-bent on targeting me.

'Danny's cheated on her a couple of times,' Bea told me.

'She's just incredibly insecure and was never able to confront the girls he cheated on her with. I guess you were the next best option for her.'

It sounds stupid. After all she's put me through these last few days, I can't help feeling sorry for her. As horrible as she was to me, she doesn't deserve that. Nobody does. I know first-hand just how easy it is for a bad relationship to tear you down until you become an unrecognisable husk of yourself.

Back in the suite, I search for her on Instagram, intending to message her and let her know that there are no hard feelings on my mind, but I quickly discover that I've been blocked.

Never mind. My sympathy is capped.

'Earth to Bailey.'

A balled-up pair of socks hit me slap-bang in the middle of my forehead. '*Hey.*'

Cash laughs and expertly dodges the return fire. 'Did you hear what I said?'

'No.'

He rolls his eyes. 'We need to go on a date.'

I crawl over to him and lay my head in his lap. His fingers come up instinctively to run through my hair. 'Hasn't this whole week essentially just been one long date?'

'I suppose. But I still want to take you on a date. As amazing as this has all been, it's not how I planned to make you mine.'

'Oh?' I quirk a brow. My heart flips at his casual use of the word *mine*. 'You've had a plan?'

'At least ten years in the making.'

Ten years.

I can't believe we've missed out on ten years of this. My mind plays back every wasted moment from the last decade of our lives. How many times have I looked at him, thinking there was only dislike and irritation bubbling under his surface when it's really been love the entire time? I feel like an idiot. I *am* an idiot.

'Hey.' Cash's hand slides along my jaw, tilting my head up to face him. 'What're you thinking?'

'Thinking about you,' I say, and my honesty surprises me. I have no filter with Cash. Not anymore.

'Oh.' He wiggles his brows. 'Bedroom thoughts?'

I roll my eyes and shove him slightly with my shoulder. 'Keep your head out of the gutter, please. I'm thinking about you. I'm thinking about us.'

'What about us?' His voice is soft.

'About how easy this all feels,' I say quietly. I link our fingers together and hold our hands in the air to make my point. 'Why is that?'

'Because we're good together,' Cash says simply. He pulls my hand towards his mouth and kisses it. 'Does that scare you?'

'A little bit,' I admit. 'It's never felt this easy – this *right* – for me before. Not with Ethan. Not with anyone.'

I know that hindsight is everything, but looking back on my two years with Ethan, I can't remember ever feeling this content or safe with him.

'Why is that a problem?'

'It's not,' I say. My brows knit in the middle. I'm frustrated that I can't get the right words out. 'I just feel like we've wasted so much time. All this time, we could've been together. We could've been *us*. I don't know. I just feel like an idiot for missing it all these years.'

'Hey.' He pulls me onto his lap, snaking his arms around my waist. '*You* didn't miss anything. If anything, this is on me. If I'd said something, you never would've spent years thinking I hated you.'

'In that case, let's agree to blame Dane.'

He laughs, rocking forward slightly as his head dips into my neck. 'I can get behind that.' He pulls back, his gaze turning serious. 'Don't overthink this, okay?'

'Okay,' I agree.

His lips quirk upwards into a grin that's more sly than anything else as he scooches back on the bed until his back hits the headboard. He presses his lips against mine, and his hands begin to wander. They leave a fiery trail in their wake as they dart under the hem of my T-shirt, and I grin into our kiss. I'm not going to waste any more time.

I know what I've got in front of me now, and I don't plan on letting it go.

Chapter Twenty-One

The sky above London is overcast and grey, but I still feel like I've got the warmth of the Jamaican sun on me as Cash and I drag our suitcases through the busy airport.

I remember how I felt just seven days ago. How nervous and anxious I was to approach the check-in counter, not even entirely sure that Cash would be there waiting for me. I remember how certain I was that Cash couldn't stand me, that I was his absolute least favourite person in the entire world and that he was doing this only as a favour to Dane.

And now here he is, standing by my side, and he's not going anywhere.

I'm his, and he's mine.

The thought brings a smile to my lips, which immediately disappears as I spot a head of familiar blonde hair in front of me.

True to her word, Penelope kept Lacey and Danny away

from the rest of us for the last few hours of the trip. I'd assumed they'd been put on an earlier flight as they didn't even leave the resort with us, but I can see Lacey stomping ahead of us now, a fierce scowl fixed on her face. Danny is nowhere to be seen, and that annoying twinge of guilt stirs up in me again.

'Don't worry about her,' says Cash, as if he can read my thoughts.

'Is it weird that I feel bad for her?'

'No. Not for you,' he says. 'You're a good person. Me, on the other hand . . .' He trails off ominously, and I can't stop the snort of laughter that erupts from me. 'I'm just saying,' he continues. 'Not everyone deserves your sympathy.'

He's right. Lacey doesn't deserve it. She refused to give me even an inch of grace, deciding to push forward with her warped idea of me instead. Why do I owe her anything else?

I hold my head high as we pass her in the crowd and successfully resist the urge to turn around and see if she's noticed us.

We make our way to the taxi rank, and as we wait in the queue for one to become available, I pull out my phone. I've got a bunch of notifications from Instagram, but I don't click on them just yet. Instead, I open up my chat with Amber.

> **AMBER**
> Have you landed yet?
>
> EXCUSE ME HAVE YOU LANDED YET???
>
> omg don't make me get on a train to Gatwick to find out myself
>
> BAILEY! ARE YOU HOME??

I press the FaceTime button, and within seconds her smiling face fills the screen.

'You're home!' she says, her voice a half-whisper. 'How was the flight?'

'Not too bad,' I say. 'Where *are* you?' I know she's only been living in her new place for a couple of weeks, but this definitely doesn't look like the bedroom she's sent videos of. It's darker, bigger, and— My eyes widen as a muscled arm suddenly drapes over her front. '*Amber.*'

She bites her lip to smother the giggle that's desperate to come out. 'Yeah. I need to update you on some *developments*.' Then it's her turn for her eyes to widen as Cash pops his head over my shoulder. 'Seems like you do too?' She nods at Cash. 'Caspian.'

Cash nods back, lips twitching in amusement. 'Amber.'

Before I can say anything, the owner of the muscled arm around her waist groans and tries to pull her over to his side of the bed. Amber shoots me a wink. 'We'll talk later.'

'Who was that with her?' Cash asks, sounding amused.

'Pretty sure that's Asshole Client,' I tell him. 'Also known as Stupidly Handsome Dickhead.'

He laughs at the nicknames. 'Ouch.'

A taxi soon arrives for us, and we climb into it. Cash immediately relays my parents' address to the driver, and then we're off, hurtling down the motorway and heading back to reality.

Returning to my parents' house after all this doesn't bother me as much as I thought it would. I don't feel like I'm returning as a failure. I've got an idea of where I want my career to go, and I know how I want to get there. It might take a while, but I'll get there. This is just a temporary stop for me now, and the light at the end of the tunnel is a little easier to see.

I pull out my phone again and launch Instagram. Just the few snippets of the trip I've already posted have done wonders for my engagement levels.

I'm sitting at 235,456 followers, and my numbers are still steadily climbing. I feel a sense of hope that I've not felt towards my job during these last few months. It's going to be a rocky road, but I'm confident that I can do it.

This is what I do, and I'm good at it.

I no longer feel that familiar bubble of anxiety in the pit of my stomach as I open up my camera roll and choose a handful of photos to post.

'How about one of these?' I show Cash my phone and swipe across to one of the photos we took the night of our candlelit dinner on the beach. I'd assumed that none of the photos had turned out well because I didn't get the kiss I was gunning for, but I'm left pleasantly surprised. In the one I've chosen, I'm smiling at the camera, but Cash's head is tilted downwards, and he's staring directly at me. Even in the low light, the sunset behind us covering us in a pinkish-purple glow, I can see *want* in his eyes.

I swipe to the next photo. In this one, we're both looking at each other, and there's something heartbreakingly fragile in our gaze. Like, in that moment, we both know we're on the precipice of something huge, but we're both too scared to take the next step.

I'm so glad that we did.

'Seeing you in that dress again . . .' Cash shifts in his seat, subtly trying to adjust himself. He swallows, and when he looks at me, I see that *want* reflected in his eyes again. His hand comes up to rest on my knee, and even through the thick fabric of my sweatpants, his touch leaves a scorching wake. I reflexively glance forward and meet the taxi driver's eyes in the rear view mirror for half a second before he darts his gaze away.

I put my hand over Cash's and give him a squeeze. 'Not now,' I murmur.

Cash makes an irritated sound low in his throat but nods

in agreement. He leans down and steals a kiss. It's hot, his tongue darting past my lips to caress my own, and filled with the promise of more to come. When we reluctantly pull away, he keeps his hand on my knee and turns his attention back to my phone. 'Post that one.'

He chooses the one where we're both looking at each other, and I agree. I scan through the rest of my camera roll and choose a handful of photos and videos to post. Cash features heavily in most of them, and so do the others. I purposely chose the selfie we took together in the bathroom that first night. Bea, Meera and Sara are squashed up beside me, wide grins tugging at their lips as we all pose for the camera. Looking at it now, you'd never be able to tell that I was in such a terrible state only minutes before the photo was taken.

I pool my selection of photos into one carousel post and make the photo of Cash and me the first one. I tag everyone in the photos, including Cash, and then type a quick caption.

Jamaica ♥ *Seven days can change your life*

And then I hit *post*.

Epilogue

CASH

I have been in love with Bailey Clarke since we were teenagers. I'm two days away from my thirtieth birthday, and the realisation hits me like a truck.

Bailey is lying sprawled across my chest, one bare leg slung over my waist, the other tangled with one of my own beneath the sheets. Her hair is a mess, sticking up in every direction, her face is flushed, and her lips are parted in a small 'o' as she snores quietly. She shifts suddenly, taking the blankets with her. I'm treated to a wonderful view of the curve of her breast as a soft groan spills from her lips. She nuzzles her head closer to my chest, as if she can't get close enough.

I know the feeling.

I have been in love with Bailey Clarke since we were teenagers, and sometimes I still can't believe that she's mine.

One Week in Paradise

I glance around our bedroom. Two large suitcases are waiting by the door, and there's a pile of clothes that didn't quite make the cut in the corner. I'm still getting used to calling it *our* bedroom, but it feels right, like it's always been ours. Bailey moved in two months ago, and our room, once a blank canvas, is filled with little touches of her.

Her hair products litter our cabinet space, and her clothes are draped haphazardly across any surface available. Our walls are covered in memories – photos of us over the course of the last nine months, starting with that trip to Jamaica.

I reach a hand out and ghost it down her side, enjoying the way her lips twitch upwards into a subconscious grin. She arches her body into my touch, and I wonder when I'll finally get used to this. Waking up to find her snoring gently against my chest, our legs tangled together, warm skin against even warmer skin.

I feel like I'm waiting for someone to come and tear the carpet out from underneath me. But they never come.

Thank God.

I don't have the words to explain how much I'm enjoying the life we're building together. Bailey's career is soaring in ways she never even suspected. She's carved her own little niche amongst the thousands of influencers all trying to get a piece of the pie and now has her own podcast she runs with Bea – B-Squared: a sex, relationships and lifestyle podcast. I don't know how she balances it all – recording the podcast, creating videos and content for the never-ending stream of brands in her inbox, but she does, and she makes it look easy.

Bailey stretches, and her eyes flutter open. For a moment or two, she stares at me, blinking away the last vestiges of sleep. Then her smile widens, and she leans up and presses her lips against mine.

It'll be very easy for this to turn into something else. For our soft, fleeting kisses to quickly turn fervent as our hands map their way across our bodies.

We've spent the last nine months learning each other's bodies, getting this intimate dance down to a science. She knows just what to do with her hands, and lips, and tongue – *oh God, her fucking* tongue – to bring out the kind of moans that come from the very depths of my throat. She knows which way to angle her hips to make my eyes roll back and a guttural moan pour from my mouth.

She knows exactly what to do to pull me apart and piece me back together again.

But we don't have time for that today.

Her sigh is laced with irritation when I reluctantly pull away from her.

'Good morning, babe.'

'It *was* a good morning,' she says. She cups my jaw and tries to pull my face back in, but I grab her wrists and hold her in place.

'We've got an hour before we need to leave,' I tell her.

Realisation dawns on her, and the irritation in her eyes melts away, leaving space for excitement to flood in. She rolls away from me and jumps out of bed.

'Any more guesses?' she asks as she grabs one of my T-shirts from the floor and yanks it over her head.

I shake my head. My birthday is in two days, and she's been planning this trip for the last few months. She's been uncharacteristically tight-lipped about it all, and the only clue she's given me is *'bring sun cream'* which doesn't exactly narrow down our options.

She grins, far too pleased with herself, and I swear to God I fall in love with her all over again.

'Good.' She bounces back to the bed. The hem of my T-shirt barely covers her ass, and I'm tempted to just say fuck it all and pull her back into bed with me. But she's been working hard planning this trip, and I don't want to see her hard work go to waste.

I settle for one last chaste kiss, laced with promises of what's to come, and then let her go. She disappears into the bathroom, and I reluctantly peel myself out of bed.

I won't lie. I'm excited about the trip, but the prospect of getting on a plane again doesn't fill me with joy. But I'll do it for her. Anything to see that smile on her face.

We get dressed and are ready to leave the apartment in record time. If Bailey senses my trepidation about boarding a plane again, she doesn't mention it. She's practically buzzing with anticipation and excitement as we head downstairs and enter the black taxi waiting for us outside.

'Where to?' the driver asks once we're settled inside.

I look over at Bailey, and she's almost bouncing she looks so excited. I expect her to direct the driver to Heathrow or Gatwick Airport, but instead, she says, 'Southampton Port, please.'

Southampton Port?

'Mhm,' she hums, leaning into me as the taxi pulls off. 'Southampton Port.'

My brain is a second or two too slow, but it eventually catches up as I connect the dots. 'We're going on a cruise?'

'We're going on a cruise!' she echoes, eyes dancing with delight as she takes in my reaction. 'To the Cayman Islands.'

'A *cruise*?'

'Yes, a cruise. Keep up, babe.'

I can't believe it. I've been psyching myself up to get on a plane for her. Meanwhile, she's been planning a goddamn *cruise* for me.

'I know you don't like planes,' she says softly. She puts her hand on my knee and gives me a squeeze. 'And I wanted you to enjoy this trip right from the beginning.'

'Bailey. Thank you.'

'You don't have to thank me.' She looks up at me through her lashes. 'I wanted to do this for you. I love you, Cash.'

The first time she told me she loved me, about three months after we returned from Jamaica, it came as a shock. I don't think either of us had been expecting it when the words came out off-handedly after dinner one night. She's repeated the phrase countless times since then, but I'll never tire of hearing it.

Each time she says it, her eyes light up, and the corners of her lips twitch upwards into a content smile. She means it. She really does.

Bailey Clarke loves *me*.

I capture her lips with mine. 'I love *you*, Bailey.'

She kisses me back eagerly, greedily giving just as much as she takes.

'How long is the cruise for?' I ask when we finally pull apart.

'Fourteen days.' She slots perfectly into my side, head resting on my shoulder.

'Seven days in Jamaica got us here,' I say. 'Where do you think we'll be after fourteen days?'

She sighs, sounding happy and content. 'I don't know, but I can't wait to find out.'

Acknowledgements

First and foremost, I want to say the biggest thank you of my life to all the readers who took a chance on me during my self-publishing journey. When I first started floating the idea of putting my writing out into the world and seeing if anyone liked it, I never would've imagined I'd end up here, and it's truly thanks to all your phenomenal support that we're at this stage. I am eternally grateful.

I also want to say thank you to my writer friends who have provided endless hours of support and love in our group chats over the years. You are all a beacon of inspiration. To my real-life friends and family who may not know my pen name but are forever tickled by the fact that I have an alter ego who writes sweet and spicy romances, I love you all! Thank you for being supportive even without knowing the full story ;)

A special shoutout to my husband, whose unwavering

support has been my rock. You always believe in me, and I'm endlessly grateful.

I owe a huge thank you to the team at S&S for seeing something special in my writing and taking a chance on me. Molly, your faith has opened doors I never dreamed possible.

And to my amazing agent, Emma, thank you for being the best champion anyone could ask for. Thank you for believing in me even when I didn't believe in myself.

Do you want to find out more?

Scan the QR code to get an extra spicy bonus chapter by signing up to Anise's newsletter.

If you enjoyed Bailey and Cash's story, read on for a sneak peek of the second book in the Flights and Feelings series.

ONE LAST JOB

Chapter One

AMBER

The walls are green. No, that's not quite right. The walls are *apple* green.

I turn around and hold up two paint swatches. In my left hand, *apple* green. In my right, *rye* green. Ricardo, one of my contractors, shoots me a nervous grimace as I shake the two swatches in front of his face. I like Ricardo. He's good at what he does, efficient, and, most importantly, he treats me with respect and makes sure his employees do too. We've never had any problems before. Until now.

Because the walls are *apple* green and the client requested *rye*.

'Come on, Ric,' I groan. 'Tell me what happened here.' We're forty-eight hours away from install day, and the last thing I need to see right now are apple green walls in the master bedroom.

'I'm so sorry, Amber. I've got a new apprentice working

with me and I thought he'd be able to handle this room alone.' He runs a hand down his face and shakes his head. 'It's my fault. I should've checked in on him more often. I take full responsibility.'

I reach for my hair and twist a few strands around my finger. The action helps to ground me, stops me from entering a never-ending anxiety spiral as apple green walls close in on me.

'Do you think the client will notice? They do look very similar.'

The laugh that bursts from my lips is borderline hysterical. *Yes*, the client is going to notice. I spent a painstaking three hours going back and forth on the pros and cons of apple versus rye with the client, and they were adamant about going with the latter.

And the colours don't look similar. Not at all.

To the untrained eye they might look identical, but there are yellow undertones in the rye green to help brighten the room, and that's why we chose it. The apple green, as beautiful a colour as it is, is too warm for a room like this and does absolutely nothing for the space.

'It's okay,' I say. But it's not. We're on a tight deadline with this project, and the client is expecting their dream home to be available to them in two short days. So yeah. Definitely not okay. 'How long will it take to repaint?'

'I can have it ready by this time tomorrow.'

I chew the inside of my cheek. Not ideal. 'If you can have it done by 10am tomorrow, I'll pretend like this never happened.'

Ricardo's face is a portrait of relief. I know he relies on the work my company gives him — we pay well, and the work is relatively steady. 'Got it, boss.'

Thankfully, the other rooms have all been painted correctly.

It needs a good clean, but aside from a few tiny scratches on the hardwood floors in the living room — which Ricardo assures me will easily be dealt with before he leaves today — the rest of the house is ready.

I lean against the banister and exhale the breath I've been keeping sucked in throughout my tour of the home. *We're nearly there.* I pull out my phone and fire off a quick email to my ware house manager, Simon, giving him the go-ahead to start loading the trucks for install day. Knowing that we're nearly there, that the finish line is offcially in sight, should help to ease some of the pressure I feel, but it doesn't.

There's still so much to do.

I still need to send over a final list to Simon and his team to double-check that every item is included and packed securely onto the trucks. I also need to head back to the office and print off floor plans for each room, then come *back* to the house and make sure they're pasted everywhere so nobody has any excuse for putting things in the wrong places.

I glance at my watch and groan. It's 4pm I can send Simon the list while I'm on the move, but the floor plans will have to wait until tomorrow. I've got a meeting with another client — at 5.30pm on a Wednesday.

Who does that?

Even as I ask myself the question, I know the answer.

Cynthia Zensi does that. My mentor, my boss, the founder of Zensi Designs, and the current bane of my life. Well, one of them.

When I first started at Zensi Designs nearly seven years ago as an assistant, Cynthia had been a completely different person. She was an icon in the British design space with a reputation for creating elegant, sophisticated and timeless interiors for her bursting little black book full of elite clients. She was a trend-setter Innovative, bright, and bold.

And she was my idol.

I devoured every piece of information imaginable I could find about her, fervently collecting magazine profiles and touring the country to visit the spaces she designed. I remember spending the day in the lobby of a hotel she designed in Scotland just after I turned eighteen, marvelling at her skill, her vision, her talent.

Three years later, and fresh from university, it felt like destiny when she announced unexpectedly that she was looking for an assistant. I spent a full week working on my application, crafting the perfect cover letter, and putting together the perfect portfolio; I felt sick when I finally hit Send. The next three weeks passed in a blur of nail-biting and refreshing my inbox every few minutes and miraculously ended with an invitation to interview. I ultimately beat out hundreds of applicants and earned the job as *Cynthia Zensi's* assistant.

Sometimes I wish I could go back in time and capture the essence of excitement, joy and trepidation I had back on my first day of work, just to remember what it felt like. Seven years on and there's no trace of it anymore. Cynthia has managed to slowly suck the life out of the one thing that has ever really brought me any happiness.

Though, to be fair, she's sucked it out of herself as well.

Seven years and two messy divorces later, the Cynthia I once looked up to no longer exists. She's a shell of her former self, and I can't remember the last time she actually worked on a project. These days, she just palms them off on me, though she's more than happy to take the credit.

Her name still holds considerable weight in the design world, but that's only because of me. I've been single-handedly managing all of Cynthia's high-profile clients for the last few years, keeping the business afloat while Cynthia swans around doing God knows what. Everyone seems to believe that she's still behind the scenes working hard and that I'm just her conduit, but they're all my designs.

My ideas.

My vision.

But on paper, I'm still a *junior* designer, and nothing I do seems to convince her to give me the promotion and the title we both know I deserve.

So it doesn't surprise me in the slightest that she's locked in a meeting for me with a high-profile client at 5.30pm on a Wednesday.

It does piss me off though.

★ ★ ★

In the middle of rush hour, it takes me just over an hour to make it to the West End. I'm still early for the meeting, but only just. I used my time on the tube, squashed between businessmen and school kids in dire need of deodorant, to draft my nal list for Simon and study up on this new client.

I've got to hand it to Cynthia. She may not be working properly anymore, but she still knows how to pull in the most lucrative clients. I'm meeting with someone called Finn Hawthorne. He's the managing director of The August Room, a private members club that was founded in New York nearly fifty years ago. It's got a reputation as being one of the most exclusive and glamorous private clubs in the world, and they're looking to branch out to new locations. Apparently, London is the first place they've chosen for their expansion.

One Last Job

They've purchased a stunning Georgian townhouse in the centre of the West End, and Cynthia has earned us the contract to design it.

I feel a tiny bubble of excitement as I scan through the photos of the building. It's a truly remarkable space with four floors, each ripe for a redesign. Most of my recent projects have been residential, which is fun and all, but *this*? This is a real challenge, something I can sink my teeth into and really flex my design muscles. It's a listed property, so it'll be a tricky project because I'll have to be creative to make sure we don't break any rules about maintaining the property's historical integrity, but everything about this excites me.

Maybe I won't complain about Cynthia foisting *this* client on me.

The townhouse is about a ten-minute walk from the nearest tube station, and I join the rush hour madness as we file down the crowded London streets. I'm going through some preliminary ideas for the property in my mind, when a voice cuts through my thoughts.

It's coming from a man a few paces in front of me. I can't see his face, but he's tall with a rower's physique hidden under his navy blue blazer, and he has a head of short blond hair. He's on the phone, his voice — loud, deep, and distinctly American — cutting through the noise of the city around us.

'. . . landed a couple hours ago. Yeah. Pretty cold. Yeah. Yeah. Uh huh. Exactly.'

I try to tune him out, my focus on the Google Maps route I'm following on my phone, but his next sentence pulls me back in.

'... meeting with the designer now.' A pause and a low chuckle. 'That's what I'm saying. You should see how much they've quoted.' Another pause. Several hums. 'Exactly. It's ridiculous. All that for choosing a couple of shades of paint and picking out a few pillows at IKEA?' He laughs loudly at something the person on the other end says, and I can't help but scowl at his back.

His attitude toward my career is, sadly, not an uncommon one. Annoyingly, it's one that my parents have too. Maybe that's why his words feel like a personal attack on me.

When it comes to interior design, people only see the finished product — a beautifully designed space — and assume that all we've done is throw some paint on the walls and maybe artfully place a rug here or there. Or they watch one of those sixty-minute design shows on daytime TV and think that entire home renovations can be done in an hour.

They don't see the hours and hours of work we put in behind the scenes: creating floor plans, managing contractors and warehouses, sourcing items, hauling around furniture only for the client to turn their nose up at it at the very last minute.

It's hard fucking work.

'... yeah, I'm going to see if I can get the price down at this ...'

He trails off and I lose him as he makes a sharp turn and dips inside a coffee shop.

Good riddance.

I wish I knew which designer he's about to meet. I'd get in touch and warn them that they've got an asshole client coming their way.

The rest of the short walk is blissfully free of assholes, and by the time I reach the listing, I've mostly pushed him from my mind.

The townhouse is as stunning up close as it was in the pictures. The four floors tower over me, and I marvel at the beautiful façade made from greying stone. Whoever the previous owners were, it's clear that they took great care of it. I step under the portico, held up by four stone columns, and lift the large circular knocker. It swings against the door with a loud *bang*, announcing my arrival.

I wait, expecting the door to open any second now. But it doesn't. I knock again, a little harder this time, and wait. And wait.

And wait.

And *wait*.

I glance at my watch, irritation practically seeping into my bloodstream. 5.45pm. He's late. This doesn't bode well for the project.

I'm about five seconds away from pulling my phone out and trawling through my emails to find some contact details for this Finn Hawthorne — and proof that Cynthia *did* actually schedule this appointment — when a voice catches my attention.

It's loud, deep, and distinctly American.

'Amber? Amber Wyatt from Zensi Designs?'

I glance over my shoulder. There's a man striding towards me. He's tall — six feet four at *least* — and even in my heels, I can tell he'll be head and shoulders over me. He's shed the blazer, opting to hang it loosely from one arm. In his other hand he's holding a paper cup with a coffee shop logo pasted across the front wrapper.

Realisation dawns on me.

Oh no.

God, please no.

He grins at me as he steps underneath the portico and offers me his coffee-free hand. 'Finn Hawthorne from The August Room. Sorry I'm late, but it's lovely to meet you.'

| NEWS & EVENTS | BOOKS | FEATURES | COMPETITIONS |

Follow us online to be the first to hear from your favourite authors

Join our mailing list for the latest news, events and exclusive competitions

Sign up at
booksandthecity.co.uk